The Lies We Tell

Fall From Grace
Book 2

Beth Orsoff

ISBN: 979-8-9887329-1-4 (paperback)

www.bethorsoff.com

Also by Beth Orsoff:

Chapter 1

THIS WAS the second time in my life I was entering the iron gates of the Wellstone Center. The first time I arrived in the back of an ambulance. Today I drove through the entrance in my own car, but my heart was still pounding so hard it felt like it was going to burst through my chest.

My first visit to the Wellstone Center had been nearly six months ago when I was admitted on a seventy-two-hour involuntary hold. Back then I hated everything about the place. Today, as a visitor instead of a patient, I could at least appreciate the facility's beautiful park-like grounds.

The only person in the world for whom I would voluntarily return to the Wellstone Center was MJ. He and his sister Sofia needed a ride. Today was their first visit with their mother since she'd left their apartment six months ago and never returned. After Maria was arrested for drug possession with intent to sell, she was given a choice between jail or rehab. That's how she ended up at the Wellstone Center. Once she detoxed, they moved her to the Wellstone Center's residential facility where she was allowed to have visitors. When I arrived at the Wellstone Center after my failed suicide attempt, I'd been housed in a different wing of the complex, but all the programs shared the same grounds.

I checked us in at the front desk, then sat with MJ and Sofia on the patio while we waited for their mother to appear. I wasn't sure Maria would want to meet me. I didn't know how much she'd been told but, surely, she knew I had forged a relationship with her children and I saw them whenever I wanted. That fact alone might make her hate me. If she also knew at one time I'd enquired about terminating her parental rights and adopting MJ and Sofia, that would seal the deal.

But my plans had never progressed that far. I had to foster before I could adopt, and that's where my plan hit a snag. The State of California doesn't allow people who recently attempted suicide to become foster parents, go figure. Which is how my Aunt Maddy had ended up becoming MJ and Sofia's foster parent instead of me. My plan worked well for a while until Maria resurfaced and the whole thing blew up.

MJ and Sofia had new foster parents now. Tim and Richard fostered four other children in addition to MJ and Sofia, so they knew how the system worked. Tim and Richard were loving foster parents, the kind they made movies about. Although I guessed they made movies about the other kind of foster parents too. Just different movies.

But with so many kids to care for Tim and Richard never had enough time. They were thrilled when I offered my help, which is how I ended up driving MJ and Sofia to the Wellstone Center today. Tim and Richard were so appreciative of my assistance they routinely invited me over to their house. And I loved spending time there. With six kids, two dogs, one cat, and a gecko, their home was always lively. And loud. Which meant, as much as I enjoyed being there, I was always happy when the evening ended, and I could return to my own quiet house. The constant chaos of their home made me appreciate living alone again.

Yes, I was living on my own again. After MJ and Sofia moved out of my aunt's house, I did too. I still missed my husband Jonah and my daughter Amelia every single day—it was a loss I knew I'd never get over. But having grown up as an only child, I was used to spending time alone and I sometimes craved that solitude. Plus, living in my house again gave me more time to search for whatever Jonah had been up to before he died.

Ever since my aunt found the flash drive taped to the bottom of the diaper caddy, I'd been trying to unlock it. Jonah had password protected the damn thing, so I still had no idea what was on it. I'd spent endless hours trying to guess his password, without success. I'd also spent entire days scouring the house for a scrap of paper where Jonah might've written the password down. No luck so far, but I was not giving up. I'd never give up.

My therapist Dr. Rubenstein thought I was using the flash drive as a way to distract myself from dealing with my grief. Occasionally, I entertained the notion that she was right, but it never stuck. So, I routinely vacillated between thinking Jonah was perfect and I'd never meet a man that wonderful again and believing my dead husband was a deceitful bastard and our whole marriage had been a sham. But I never stopped aching for Amelia. Over time my memory of the sleepless nights, the steady stream of spit-up, and the nonstop crying faded and all I remembered was my overwhelming love for her and my grief at her loss.

But I knew from experience dwelling on the past was not good for my mental health, so I pushed thoughts of Jonah and Amelia aside and tried to be mindful and focus on the present. I took a deep breath and inhaled the scent of freshly mowed grass and focused my gaze on the tree line which acted as a barrier between the Wellstone Center's lawn and the steep hillside that led to the freeway below. Beyond the trees I glimpsed the hills on the opposite side of the freeway, which six months ago had been charred and barren from the fires but were now covered in California's ubiquitous coastal sage scrub.

I've never liked sage scrub. It's too, well, scrubby looking. I prefer soft, papery bougainvillea, which is equally ubiquitous in Southern California despite it not being a native plant. Although to be fair to sage scrub, the pink and purple hued bougainvillea were pretty, but when the rains came, those flowers were useless. It was the ugly sage scrub that kept the mudslides at bay—at least until the fires burned it all away. But the sage scrub always grew back.

That seemed like a metaphor for something, although I didn't know what. *Life finds a way?* Nah, that was a line from *Jurassic Park*, which I re-watched last night with Tim and Richard and four of the kids. We'd waited until the two youngest children went to bed because Richard thought watching dinosaurs devour people might scare them. These kids had probably seen worse in their real lives, but I didn't say so.

I was still thinking about the movie when the door to the Wellstone Center swung open and two women walked out onto the patio.

"Mama!" Sofia shouted and ran to the woman not wearing a white lab coat.

Chapter 2

Sofia threw her arms around her mother's waist, and Maria bent down and buried her face in her daughter's dark, silky hair. Maria was wearing baggy gray sweatpants and a white T-shirt that hung loosely on her gaunt frame, and I wondered if they were her own clothes or something the Center had given her from the lost and found box. I would never have recognized Maria from the photos MJ had shown me of their family in happier times, but standing next to Sofia, I could see the resemblance.

MJ stood up from the bench, but he didn't rush to Maria's side. He ambled over and stopped a few feet away.

Maria smiled at him with tears, I presumed, of joy, sliding down her cheeks. When MJ didn't move, she opened one arm wide, keeping the other firmly around Sofia's shoulder, and said, "*Mijo*, I missed you so much."

"I missed you too, Mama," he replied, but stood his ground.

That's when I left the bench and joined them on the patio. "Go hug your mother," I whispered to MJ. When he didn't immediately move, I nudged his shoulder. "Now."

He shuffled to his mother's side, allowing her to embrace

him. She had to stand on her toes to kiss his cheek. Eventually, she stopped fussing over her children and turned her attention to me.

"I'm Grace." I smiled. "I'm a friend of MJ's." That seemed the easiest way to describe our current relationship.

Maria gave me a dubious look and turned to her son.

"She's teaching me to be a lawyer, Mama."

"A lawyer?" She said something to him in Spanish, which I didn't understand.

That's when the woman in the lab coat, who'd been standing off to the side watching the exchange, offered me her hand. "Cheryl Simpson. I'm a family therapist here at the Center."

"Grace Keegan Hughes," I said as I shook her hand.

"Will you be the one bringing the kids to visit?" she asked, clearly confused about my role here.

"No, I just drove them today because their foster parents were busy."

"Then you're not their legal guardian?"

"No," I said without elaboration.

"Okay, well, they'll be meeting with their mom for about an hour today, depending on how things go. First visits are always a little unpredictable. Were you planning on waiting here or were you going to leave and come back? I can text you when they're done."

There was no nearby coffee shop, and by the time I drove home, I'd just have to turn around and drive back, so I told her I'd wait. It was too hot to loiter on the sunny patio, so I decided to take a walk around the grounds.

I'D JUST SETTLED onto a patch of grass under a large shady tree trying to clear my mind and meditate, when I heard a voice calling my name. I opened my eyes and spied Dr. Stetler heading towards me. If I'd spotted him before he'd spotted me, I would've hidden. Too late now. He was wearing the same khakis he'd worn every day I'd been a patient at the Wellstone Center, but in a nod to the weather, he'd paired the pants with a short-sleeve button down instead of his signature flannel shirt.

I'd been sitting cross-legged, but as he approached, I stretched my legs out in front of me, ensuring there would be at least a few feet of distance between us and he'd have to stand in the sun. "How long have you been here?" he asked, shading his eyes from the glare.

I glanced up. "Under this tree? Just a few minutes."

The smile remained plastered on his face, but I could tell from the deep breath he drew in then slowly released that my answer had annoyed him. Mission accomplished.

"Same old Grace," he said.

"Yup," I replied, but it wasn't true. When I'd arrived at the Wellstone Center after my failed suicide attempt, I'd wanted to die. Now I was committed to living. And Dr. Stetler deserved none of the credit for the change in my mental state.

"So, you're back as an outpatient?" he asked.

"No, just visiting." That was all the explanation I was willing to give.

"But you're still seeing a therapist, I hope."

"Yes. She's very good."

"Wonderful to hear," he said with false cheer. "Well, if you ever need me, you know where to find me."

I smiled benignly. *As if!* That's what happened when you spent your days talking to teenagers; you picked up their expressions. Olivia Baylor, my client and MJ's student since he started tutoring her in math a few months ago, said "as if" all the time. MJ picked up the expression from Olivia and now I said it too.

Olivia was the reason MJ had agreed to apply to the

Winston Academy. He had a crush on her, although he wouldn't admit it. I was just happy he was enrolled in a better high school.

I remained under the tree until MJ and Sofia reappeared on the patio, but with Dr. Simpson only.

"How did it go?" I asked.

I'd directed my question at MJ, but it was Dr. Simpson who answered. "Very well for a first visit."

I tried to make eye contact with MJ, but he stood with his hands in the pockets of his basketball shorts and stared at the ground.

"I'll send their social worker an email," Dr. Simpson said, "but you can let their foster parents know same time next week."

SOFIA SKIPPED BACK to the car, smiling and humming to herself, but MJ didn't speak. Nor did he participate in the eye-spy game Sofia and I played for the entire forty-minute drive back to Tim and Richard's house. When we arrived, I parked out front and walked them inside. I knew Tim was home because his minivan was in the driveway, but the only child with him was Makeyla. The three boys were out somewhere with Richard.

"How did it go today?" Tim asked, glancing from MJ to me.

I met Tim the day after Sofia and MJ had moved in. MJ had texted me his new foster home was okay, but I wanted to see for myself. And I had an excuse to visit because I'd promised to drop off Sofia's dollhouse. Tim was tall and broad shouldered with freckled skin and a wholesome smile. I immediately imagined him as a former prom king who'd dated cheerleaders in high school and was the star of the football team. I could not have been more wrong.

Tim had helped me carry the dollhouse in from my car, then offered me a coffee. I accepted and we ended up talking for hours. That's when I learned he knew from a young age he was gay and he hated sports. Richard, his husband, was the sports fan in the family. I met him when Tim invited me over for a barbeque that weekend. With his dark skin, dad bod, and prickly demeanor, Richard was the inverse of Tim. They were the poster couple for opposites attract.

MJ replied to Tim's question about his mother with a shrug and raced up the steps. A few seconds later we heard a bedroom door slam shut and we both stared up at the ceiling. Then Tim turned to the girls and suggested they go out back and play with the dogs. After Makeyla and Sofia left, Tim said, "I take it the visit didn't go well?"

I shrugged too. "The therapist thought it did, and Sofia seems okay, but MJ hasn't said a word."

"Hmmm," Tim replied. "Maybe he just needs time to process. It's been what, three months since he last saw his mother?"

"Six," I answered.

"That's a lot to deal with, especially at fifteen." Then Tim smiled, as if the mere act of smiling could push the bad thoughts away. Maybe for him it could. "We're taking the kids to the beach tomorrow. It's Isaiah's birthday. You want to come?"

"Ummm." Six kids at the beach did not sound like a relaxing way to spend a Sunday afternoon.

"I'm baking chocolate cake."

He knew I couldn't say no. Tim was a terrific baker.

I ARRIVED at the beach at noon, just as they were breaking out the sandwiches.

"Thank god," Tim said when he spotted the potato chips

peeking out of the top of the grocery bag. "I thought they were going to mutiny because the only snacks I brought were cucumber slices and carrot sticks."

"You deserve a mutiny for that," I said as I passed the family-sized bags of Doritos and Lays to MJ and Jayden. At seventeen, Jayden was the oldest of Tim and Richard's foster children. MJ was second oldest and the two had become friends.

I wished Isaiah a happy birthday and handed him the gift card I'd purchased this morning. I'd tried to buy him a real present. I'd spent fifteen minutes walking up and down the aisles of Target trying to guess what an eleven-year-old boy might like before I finally gave up and purchased the gift card instead.

Then I waved to Ethan and the girls, accepted a kiss on the cheek from Tim, a moist hug from Richard, whose body was wet with sweat or sea water or both, and popped open my sand chair under their shade canopy.

Tim searched inside the giant cooler. "We've got chicken pesto, vegetarian, or peanut butter and jelly. What's your pleasure?"

"Homemade pesto?" I asked. Tim's pesto was the best I'd ever eaten.

"Is there any other kind?" Tim replied.

There was at my house. Now that I was living alone again, cooking meant heating up food from a jar, a box, or a takeout container.

Tim passed a foil-wrapped sandwich to MJ. "Give this to your Lawyer Mom."

"Lawyer Mom?" I'd never heard that expression before.

MJ walked the sandwich over to me. "Janelle's my lawyer and you're my lawyer-mom."

"I thought I was your boss?"

He shrugged and returned to his beach towel.

The kids ate their sandwiches and most of the chips, then we all sang happy birthday to Isaiah and devoured Tim's cake. When all that was left was a pile of chocolate crumbs, the kids headed out into the sun again. Sofia, Makeyla, and Ethan returned to their sandcastle, and MJ, Isaiah, and Jayden ran into the surf.

Richard reached into a smaller cooler behind his beach chair and pulled out a hard seltzer.

I raised my eyebrows. "I thought alcohol wasn't allowed on the beach."

"You going to turn me in?" Richard asked.

"Not if you give me one."

Richard smiled. "Black cherry, mango, or lime?"

"Mango," I replied, and he tossed me a can. I swallowed a mouthful of the sweet, fizzy soda, leaned back in my chair, and closed my eyes. My belly was full, the ocean breeze cooled my warm skin, and the rhythmic sound of the crashing waves mixed with the din of screaming children lulled me to the edge of sleep.

Then Richard said, "Who's that chatting up MJ?" and I startled awake.

Chapter 3

I OPENED my eyes and spotted Tim craning his neck for a better view. "I don't know who MJ's talking to. I've never seen him before."

I stood up so I, too, could get an unobstructed view then quickly sat down again. "That's Mr. Guardia. He was MJ's math teacher last year."

Richard turned his attention back to his phone, but Tim's gaze remained fixed on MJ and Mr. Guardia, who were standing shoulder to shoulder in waist-deep surf. "If my math teacher looked like that, I might not have dropped calculus."

"Down boy," Richard said without looking up.

"You think he's single?" Tim asked.

"What does it matter?" Richard replied. "You're not." Then he waggled his silver banded finger at Tim, who was sporting an identical ring on his left hand.

"Not for me, you dolt, for Grace."

I choked on my seltzer. "Me?" I croaked.

"Yes, you," Tim said. "When's the last time you went on a date?"

"Need I remind you until recently I was a happily married woman?"

"Not that recently," Tim replied.

"Leave her alone," Richard said in a tone I'd previously only heard him use when one of the kids was misbehaving.

Tim dismissed him with a wave of his hand and stood up. "C'mon," he said, turning to me. "You can introduce us."

"MJ can introduce you." I was comfortable in my sand chair and had no desire to move.

Tim placed his hands on his hips. "Have you ever seen MJ do an introduction?"

I laughed thinking back to the day he'd met Olivia. I'd had to do all the talking for the first ten minutes because neither of them would say a word to the other. "Okay, okay," I said, pushing myself upright. "Just promise you won't embarrass me."

"Now why on earth would I do that?" Tim said.

The sand scorched our feet, so we ran down to the ocean. But as soon as the water splashed onto my calves, I jumped back. Even at the end of summer the Pacific Ocean was chilly. Tim called out to MJ, who was twenty feet away, and both he and Mr. Guardia turned around. They waded out of the ocean and joined Tim and me on the wet sand.

The last time I'd seen Mr. Guardia was in Principal Ramirez's office the day MJ got suspended for fighting in school. Mr. Guardia had been wearing pants and a long-sleeved shirt. Today all he was wearing was a loose-fitting bathing suit. His skin was golden brown, and his bare chest was covered in a smattering of dark hair that winnowed to a thin line down his torso before disappearing into his waistband. Yes, I noticed.

"Ms. Hughes?" Mr. Guardia seemed genuinely surprised to see me.

Tim didn't wait for an introduction. "Tim Chase," he said and extended his hand. "I'm one of MJ's foster dads."

"Daniel Guardia," he replied, shaking Tim's hand. "I was MJ's math teacher last year."

"Grace told us," Tim said, then pointed back to the canopy. "That's my husband Richard in the shade. When you're done in the water you should come and join us."

Mr. Guardia shook his head. "Thanks, but I can't."

"Why not?" Tim asked. "We've got plenty of room. You can bring whomever you're here with. The more the merrier, we always say."

I turned to Mr. Guardia. "It's true. He does always say that. That's how they ended up with six kids."

"Six?" Mr. Guardia replied, as shocked by the number as I had been.

Tim rolled his eyes. "Please tell me you're not another only child."

"No," Mr. Guardia said. "I have a brother. But I'm here alone."

"Alone?" Tim's voice rose as if coming to the beach by one's self was the most outrageous thing he'd ever heard. "Then you must join us. I insist."

MJ said, "Yeah, Mr. Guardia, you should come."

I felt bad for Mr. Guardia. He was trapped and he knew it. I smiled and said, "The food's gone, but we still have some drinks. If you ask Richard nicely, he might even share his adult beverages."

Mr. Guardia smiled back. "I guess I could come for a little while."

Mr. Guardia sat with us for the rest of the afternoon. MJ had already told him he and Sofia had moved out of my aunt's house. I explained they'd changed foster homes after their mother reappeared. Tim and Richard picked up the story from there.

The group of us spent the rest of the afternoon playing Frisbee, building the sandcastle, which had expanded into an entire kingdom, and swimming in the ocean, although they could only get me to wade in up to my knees. It wasn't until the sun started its slow descent in the sky and the kids started whining about being hungry again that Mr. Guardia said, "I really should be heading home."

"Me too," I replied.

"You're not coming back to the house for dinner?" Tim asked.

I shook my head. "Sorry, it's laundry night." I was on my last pair of clean underwear. I was also ready for some alone time. I didn't know how Richard, who was an only child too, managed. He'd told me more than once that although he loved their large family, he missed spending time alone. Tim was the youngest of five siblings and had always wanted lots of children of his own.

"Not so easy to make happen when you're a gay man," he'd confided to me one night over vodka martinis after the kids had gone to bed.

"You could always hire a surrogate." I'd worked with a gay couple in LA who'd ended up with twins that way.

"Do you know how expensive that is?" Tim had said.

I'd admitted I didn't but imagined it wasn't cheap. The couple I'd worked with were both partners at my law firm and surely made at least mid-six-figure salaries each. Probably more. "That's why you and Richard decided to become foster parents?" I'd often wondered.

"That was part of it," Tim had said. "Richard was on the fence about having kids at all, so I convinced him to foster as a sort of trial run. He's open to kids now, but he still wants a baby."

"And you don't?" I asked.

"No, I do too. But it's a lot harder to find babies who are up for adoption than older children."

Between the six kids and four adults we managed to haul the cooler, canopy, beach chairs, sand toys, and boogie boards across the hot sand and out to the parking lot. Tim and Richard had arrived early, so their minivan was parked close to the entrance. Since I hadn't shown up until noon, my SUV was at the opposite end of the parking lot.

"Do you want us to drive you to your car?" Richard asked as we loaded everything into the minivan's trunk.

"No, I'm fine." All I had to carry was my beach bag and my sand chair.

"I can walk you to your car," Mr. Guardia offered.

"Thanks, Daniel, but I'm good." I called him Daniel now because he insisted, but in my mind, he was still Mr. Guardia.

Tim said, "Grace, it's getting dark. You really shouldn't be out walking alone."

I pushed my sunglasses down the bridge of my nose and turned toward the ocean. The sun was low in the sky, but it would be at least half an hour before it sunk below the horizon. I turned back to Tim. "I think I'll be able to make it back to my car before the sun sets."

Tim gave me a meaningful look and mouthed, *Go with him,* then turned to face Mr. Guardia. "Would you mind walking Grace to her car? I'd feel better knowing she wasn't alone."

"Happy to," Mr. Guardia said.

My mind was made up for me.

Chapter 4

"SORRY ABOUT THAT," I said to Mr. Guardia, as we trudged across the sandy parking lot. He carried my chair, while I rummaged through my beach bag for my car keys.

"There's nothing to be sorry about," Daniel replied. "I offered, remember?"

"I know but..." It was obvious this was Tim's unsubtle attempt at matchmaking. Earlier in the day he'd grilled Daniel about his personal life—never married, no kids, not currently seeing anyone.

When we reached my SUV, I popped the trunk and Mr. Guardia slid my chair into the back. "Can I give you a ride to your car?" I wasn't trying to extend the conversation; I was merely being polite.

"I biked here."

"Wow, I'm impressed. How far do you live?"

"Not far," he said. "Getting to the beach is easy; it's all downhill. It's the ride home that's a workout."

"You want a ride home then?" I asked, hoping he realized all I was offering was a ride. I hadn't dated anyone since Jonah died and had no desire to.

Mr. Guardia smiled. "Sure, that'd be great."

I drove around the perimeter of the parking lot to where the bike racks were located, and Mr. Guardia jumped out. But when he tried to wedge his bike into my trunk, it didn't fit even with the rear seat laid flat. He finally pulled the bike out of the trunk and leaned it against the bumper of my SUV. "You need a bike rack."

"I would if I owned a bike."

"You don't own a bike?" he asked, incredulous.

"Not anymore." The last time I saw my bike it was hanging on the wall of my parents' garage. But that was before my dad died and my mom sold the house. I didn't know where the bike was now. My mom had probably donated it before she moved.

"But you do know how to ride a bike?" he said.

"Of course, I know how to ride a bike."

"Good. Now I know what we'll be doing on our first date."

I WAITED until I placed the last load of laundry into the dryer before I called Tim. Since we'd parted a few hours earlier he'd sent me increasingly demanding text messages wanting to know what happened with Mr. Guardia.

"Oh my god," Tim squealed when I filled him in. "Richard, did you hear that?"

"Yes," Richard replied, "she's on speakerphone, remember?"

I laughed, imagining Tim playfully smacking Richard's arm, something I'd seen him do many times.

"You said yes, right?" Tim asked.

"Yes to the date. No to the bike ride."

"Why?"

"Why to which one?"

"The bike ride," Tim said. "Obviously, you should date him."

It wasn't obvious to me. Yes, Mr. Guardia was attractive. But a lot of men are attractive. Although we'd chatted all afternoon, I didn't feel like we had any chemistry. It had been almost two years since Jonah died and my mother was constantly harping on me to "get back out there." I figured a date with Mr. Guardia would be a low stakes way to dip my toe back into the dating pool. But to Tim I just said, "Because I haven't ridden a bike since high school."

"They say you never forget," Richard called out.

"And you know what else you never forget? S-E-X," Tim stage whispered.

I laughed then hung up. I was nervous enough at the thought of going on a date again—my first in almost ten years. I didn't need to be worrying about the possibility of having sex too.

WHEN I ARRIVED at the office the next morning Janelle was already at her desk. "You look happy," she said when she saw me.

"Do I?" I tried not to smile. I'd woken up this morning from a dream of having great s-e-x with Daniel. I blamed/thanked Tim for putting the thought in my head.

"Good weekend?" she asked.

"Yes."

Janelle and I got along well, but she didn't share details about her personal life with me, so I assumed she wasn't interested in hearing about mine. The exceptions were stories about MJ and Sofia. She always wanted to hear those. For Janelle it was work-related since she still represented them. "I took the kids to see Maria on Saturday," I added.

Janelle tossed her pen onto her desk and leaned back in her chair. "And how did that go?"

I sat down in her guest chair and told her what I knew, which wasn't much. MJ had seemed happier on Sunday than he'd been on Saturday, but he hadn't mentioned his visit with Maria and I hadn't pressed him about it.

"Do you think he's changed his mind about wanting to live with her?" Janelle asked.

I considered it before I answered. "No. I think there's a part of him that's still angry with her, but at the end of the day, MJ will go where Sofia goes and Sofia was very happy to see Maria again."

"Sorry," Janelle said.

I shrugged. I hadn't expected MJ to change his mind. "In some ways I have the best of both worlds. I still see MJ all the time, but I no longer have to remind him to put his dirty clothes in the hamper and yell at him to go to bed."

She let out a laugh. "Except for the part about having to pay his tuition."

"It's only for a year." The Winston Academy had assured me MJ would be eligible for a scholarship next year if he maintained a B average. He would've been eligible this year, but he'd applied too late; all the financial aid money was already gone.

"That's more than most foster parents would do. And you're not even his foster parent."

I didn't mind. I considered it a good use of the money from Jonah's second life insurance policy. "Did you know he calls me his Lawyer Mom?"

"No, although I think a more accurate description of you would be his benefactor."

"Well, I do have great expectations."

Chapter 5

THE FOLLOWING Saturday I drove MJ and Sofia to the Wellstone Center again because Richard had promised Jayden he'd take him to a job fair and Tim was home watching the rest of the kids. My heart still raced when I drove up the Center's long driveway, but the palpitations didn't last as long as they had the week before. Again I waited with MJ and Sofia on the patio until Maria and Dr. Simpson appeared and led them inside. This time while I sat under the shade tree, I looked up from my phone every few minutes to make sure Dr. Stetler wasn't nearby.

When their visit with their mother ended and I asked MJ how it went, this time he answered me.

"S'okay. Can we get lunch? I'm starving."

I took that as a good sign.

AFTER LUNCH I drove MJ and Sofia back to Tim and Richard's house. This time both of their cars were parked in the driveway.

"Perfect timing," Tim said, as the three of us filed into the kitchen. The counter was covered with sliced bread, salad fixings, and an assortment of meats, cheeses, and condiments. "It's Make Your Own Sandwich Day."

"I'm in," MJ said, grabbing a plate.

"You just ate!" Only half an hour ago he'd wolfed down a chicken sandwich, waffle fries, and a large drink. Sofia had only eaten a handful of chicken nuggets, but she didn't want a sandwich. Instead, she headed straight for the cat, who saw her coming and hid under the sofa.

"So?" MJ said, slapping lunchmeat onto a slice of bread.

He ate more than anyone I knew, but like most teenage boys, his body burned up the calories. He was also getting taller and starting to fill out. I wasn't rail thin anymore either, but since all my clothes still fit me, I didn't feel guilty plucking a chocolate chip cookie off the dessert plate.

After each child, except Sofia who was down on her knees in the living room meowing at the cat to try to lure him out from his hiding place, had made a sandwich Richard ordered them all into the backyard with their plates. "I just vacuumed," he said apologetically. "I can't face all the crumbs again."

"Trust me, I understand. I love a clean house."

"See?" Richard said to Tim. "I'm not the only one."

"She lives alone, darling. We have six children. Clean is a concept you need to let go of." Then Tim turned away from Richard and rolled his eyes. "Tonight's the big night, right?"

"If by big night, you mean my date with Daniel, then yes."

"And what are you wearing?" Tim asked.

"I'm not sure." I'd been worrying about it all week. I'd even went shopping after work one night, but I couldn't find anything I liked. Maybe it would've helped if I knew what I was looking for. "Can I just wear pants, or do I need to wear a dress?"

"Dress," Richard said, at the same time Tim said, "Pants."

"She's got great legs," Richard told him. "She should show them off."

"A dress will make her look like she's trying too hard," Tim replied, then turned to me. "Unless he's taking you somewhere fancy."

"I have no idea where we're going." After I nixed the bike ride, I'd suggested dinner. Daniel said he'd make a reservation, but he didn't tell me where.

Tim pursed his lips. "He's a high school math teacher. I'm not thinking he's splurging for fancy on a first date. Go with business casual."

"Business casual," I said to myself as I stared at my side of the walk-in closet. I could've spread my clothes out to Jonah's side of the closet, but I hadn't. I also hadn't slept on his side of the bed.

After trying on several combinations of pants and shirts, I finally settled on dark jeans, a red silk tank top, and high heels. I'd texted Daniel earlier and offered to meet him at the restaurant—a good way to find out where we were going without having to come right out and ask—but he'd just texted me back and said he was happy to pick me up at my house unless that would make me feel unsafe. I didn't want him to think I didn't trust him, so I agreed.

Daniel arrived promptly at seven-thirty wearing gray cotton pants and a black button-down shirt. Apparently, he was going for business casual too.

"You look great," he said as I pulled the front door shut behind me.

I probably did compared to the way I'd looked at the beach. My hair wasn't in a ponytail and my face wasn't shiny from sunscreen. I was even wearing makeup and jewelry.

Daniel walked me to his car, which he'd parked next to my SUV in the driveway. *That's Jonah's spot.* Then I banished the thought from my head. "Where are we going?" I asked as he held open the passenger-side door.

"The Stoned Crab. You're not vegan or vegetarian, are you? I probably should've asked sooner."

"Nope, just allergic to seafood."

"You're kidding. I can't believe—"

I smiled. "I am kidding. I'm fine with seafood."

He stood with his hand on the door frame. "Fine with seafood. That's not the same as actually liking seafood." He pulled his phone out of his pocket and thumbed the screen as he spoke. "I don't know why I didn't ask you what kind of food you like. That was stupid of me. Let me see where else we can get in."

"Daniel, I'm great with the Stoned Crab. Really." The last time I'd eaten there was the night I'd been released from the Wellstone Center, but I'd try not to think about that.

WE WERE SEATED at a table next to the windows. Had we arrived thirty minutes earlier, we would've been able to watch the sunset. But by this hour it was already dark and the marine layer had rolled in, so the view was of a dark sky filled with clouds. We both studied our menus as if we were going to be quizzed on them. After the waiter took our order, we sipped our water and stared out at the starless sky.

"I really should've planned this better," Daniel said.

I felt sorry for him. It was obvious he was trying. He'd even ordered a ridiculously expensive bottle of wine. *Jonah would not have approved.* Then I banished thoughts of Jonah from my head.

"I used to be a planner," I said, "but not anymore. I'm much more impulsive now."

"Really?" He seemed genuinely intrigued. "Why?"

I was saved from having to answer by the waiter who brought our wine.

The alcohol helped, as it usually does. The conversation flowed more freely after we'd both consumed a glass of wine. Mostly I asked Daniel questions because I preferred listening to him talk then divulging information about myself. He told me he'd grown up in Santa Veneta but moved to northern California for college and then got a job in Silicon Valley after graduation. He'd only moved back to Santa Veneta last year.

"Were you a teacher in Silicon Valley too?"

"No, a techie."

That explained the wine. And the Tesla. I'd wondered how he could afford such an expensive car on a public-school teacher's salary. "Like Mark Zuckerberg?"

Daniel laughed and I focused on his full, pink lips and his straight white teeth. Did he whiten them or did they just look that bright because his skin was brown from the sun?

"Sorry," he said, "I'm not a billionaire. But I have met the guy."

"Really?" I'd been joking about Mark Zuckerberg. I knew some wealthy people, but they were multi-millionaires, not billionaires. "What's he like?"

He hesitated then said, "No comment."

Now I was intrigued. "What did you do in tech? Were you just a worker bee for some company or did you invent an app I'll never be able to figure out how to use?" Jonah used to tease me for being so incompetent with technology.

"Both. I created a networking app Facebook bought and promptly shutdown."

"I'm impressed. But why did they shut you down?"

"It's the Facebook way. They see purchases as talent acquisitions. I had two partners who went to work for Zuck after the sale."

25

"But not you?"

He shook his head. "I decided I needed a life change. So I came back to Santa Veneta and got a job as a math teacher."

Silicon Valley tech bro to math teacher in a public high school. There was more to this story. "That is a major life change."

Daniel topped off both of our wineglasses. "My dad had a heart attack. He survived," he quickly added, "but it caused me to reevaluate some of my decisions. It also made me realize my parents weren't getting any younger. I thought it would be nice to spend some time with them as an adult. Of course, six months after I moved back, they announced they'd sold their house and were retiring in Arizona."

I laughed. "Sorry. I know it's not funny but—"

"It's fine. I don't regret it. I like it here. It's more laid back than Silicon Valley, although it's very different than when I was a kid."

"How so?" I'd only lived in Santa Veneta for a few years.

"When I grew up here, everyone was middle class. Or, at least, that's how I remember it. I didn't know anyone who was rich or poor. It's much more economically segregated now."

"I think that's the whole country not just Santa Veneta."

"You may be right."

Then our food arrived, and the rest of the meal passed in a blur. Before I knew it, we were the last two people in the restaurant. When Daniel retrieved his car from the valet, he didn't ask me where I wanted to go. He just drove to my house and again parked in Jonah's spot in the driveway.

When he shut off the engine, I said, "Thanks for dinner. I had a nice time." Initially, I was worried because we didn't seem to have much in common. But the evening got better when we started drinking. I knew I should've stopped after I'd finished the first glass of wine, but the alcohol helped me keep thoughts of Jonah at bay.

"Me too," he said. "I'll walk you to the door."

Was he just being chivalrous or was he expecting to be invited in? I was hoping to avoid the awkward goodbye where you don't know if you're supposed to kiss or hug or not touch at all. I was so out of practice dating.

He seemed as surprised as I was when the words, "Would you like to come in?" floated out of my mouth. I immediately regretted them. I blamed it on my alcohol-soaked brain. It had been a long time since I'd drank this much.

"Sure, that'd be great."

"You don't have to," I said. "I know it's late."

"No, I want to. I definitely want to."

That made one of us. But it was too late to reverse course now. I got out of the car and led Daniel into my house.

"Whoa," he said, staring open-mouthed at the eighty-six inch television which took up most of one wall of the living room.

"Blame it on my husband." I'd mentioned Jonah and Amelia over dinner, so Daniel knew they had once existed but he didn't know much more.

"He had great taste in TVs. And women."

I looked away, embarrassed, and said the first thing that came into my head. "Do you want something to drink?"

"Sure, whatever you're having."

I hadn't planned on drinking anymore tonight. I'd drank too much already. "Would you like some coffee?"

"Sounds great."

I left him with the television, which he didn't turn on, and I returned a few minutes later with our coffees. He drank his black while I stirred milk and sugar into mine. I hadn't even taken a sip yet when he said, "I'd really like to kiss you. May I?"

The question threw me. Did people ask permission now? I guessed after Me Too they did. As with inviting him in, I didn't think and just answered reflexively. "Uh, sure."

He placed his hands, which were still warm from the coffee mug, on my shoulders and leaned in. His lips were as soft as they looked, and when his tongue touched mine, my long-dormant desire returned.

Tim was right. Some things you don't forget.

I thoroughly enjoyed kissing Daniel. The panic didn't set in until he suggested we go upstairs.

Chapter 6

"WHAT'S WRONG?" Daniel asked when I abruptly pulled away from him.

My heart was pounding so hard I wondered if he could hear it too. "Nothing," I replied. I wasn't about to explain the last time I took a man up to my bedroom the evening ended with my attempted suicide.

Daniel looked confused. "Am I misreading the signals here?"

"No."

He looked even more confused. "So...you just don't like beds? You're into other furniture?"

Now I was confused, which helped lessen my panic because it gave me something else to focus on. Had I missed the latest trend on social media? Beds were out but bathtubs or couches or kitchen tables were in? "What other furniture?"

"You tell me. I'll go wherever you want."

That sparked an idea. "How about your place?"

"My place? Now?"

"Yes."

Daniel stared at me with his mouth open. I needed to explain.

"I haven't been with anyone since my husband died and... well..." I felt a bit guilty making him think my reticence to take him to my bedroom was all about Jonah, although he was part of it. But it was just as much about Jake and the suicide attempt. I didn't think I'd ever be able to sleep with someone in that bedroom without thinking about everything else that happened in that bedroom too.

"I'm so sorry, Grace. I didn't realize. Of course, we can go back to my place."

We passed the Stoned Crab on the drive to Daniel's, and I wondered why he hadn't suggested we go back to his house to begin with. He lived much closer to the restaurant than I did.

Because he wasn't thinking you were going to sleep with him tonight.

I wasn't thinking it either until we'd started kissing. But there really was no reason to wait. Who knew what the future would bring? Carpe diem!

Don't give me that carpe diem crap. You're just terrified of sleeping with someone new and want to get it over with, preferably while drunk.

Yeah, that too.

Daniel drove up the steep hill that ran parallel to the ocean. It plateaued in the neighborhood everyone referred to as the Bluffs. The homes in this area were older than the homes in my neighborhood, but their proximity to the coastline made them much more valuable, even the ones that didn't have ocean views.

Daniel pulled into the underground garage of a low-rise condominium, and we rode the elevator to the third floor in silence. I remembered looking at a rental in this building when

Jonah and I had first moved to Santa Veneta. The complex was built in the early 1970s and I was expecting the same harvest gold kitchen countertops and ugly shag carpeting in the unit Jonah and I had viewed (and rejected). But Daniel's apartment had been completely remodeled with hardwood floors, an updated kitchen, and recessed lighting.

"This is really nice," I said, stopping at the quartz countertop breakfast bar adorned with three modern barstools.

"It's nicer in the daytime," he said. "It was the view that sold me on this place, and the fact I can ride my bike to the beach. Can I get you something to drink? Another coffee?"

I could use the caffeine since I was already getting sleepy. But my buzz was wearing off, and if I was going to go through with this, I needed more alcohol. "Do you have any wine?"

"Of course," Daniel said and headed into the kitchen. He pulled a bottle of white out of a wine refrigerator and poured two glasses. It was sweeter than the wine we'd drank at the restaurant, but it tasted good. I took my wineglass into the living room and sunk down into the buttery leather couch. Daniel followed but he didn't sit. "I'll be right back," he said, then disappeared down the hallway.

I took a long swallow of wine and tilted my head back.

I'll just close my eyes for a minute...

WHEN I OPENED MY EYES, the sky outside the living room's sliding glass door was light gray and I was curled up on the sofa, fully clothed except for my shoes, and covered with a chenille throw. I sat up and spotted the note on the coffee table.

Grace,

You fell asleep on the couch, and you looked so peaceful I didn't want to wake you. Went for a bike ride but I'll be back by eight. I'd love to take you to breakfast.

Daniel

"Oh god," I said to the empty room. How could I let this happen? I wanted to sleep with him when I was drunk so it would be less awkward. Now I was going to have to sit across from him sober and pretend we weren't both thinking the same thing?

I should just leave. If he thinks I'm rude and never calls me again, I'm okay with that.

Of course, he's going to call you again. He's going to want to finish what you started, you idiot. He's probably hoping to get lucky this morning.

I was not feeling lucky. I was feeling hungover. I located my shoes and purse on the floor next to the couch and grabbed my phone. I was still searching Uber and Lyft for the closest driver when I heard a key in the lock and the front door opened. Daniel appeared in the entranceway in black bike shorts and a matching Lycra T-shirt.

"Good morning," he said, way too cheerily. He dropped his bike helmet on the breakfast bar before moving to the open-concept living room, his cycling shoes click-clacking against the hardwood floor with each step. He stopped a few feet away from me, hands on his trim hips. "How'd you sleep?"

"I'm so sorry I fell asleep on you." For a moment I wondered if he'd drugged me, but quickly realized that was a ridiculous notion. I was the one who'd suggested we come back to his place. Plus, I was still wearing all my clothes.

"Don't be. The couch is super comfortable. I've fallen asleep on it many times." Then he turned and click-clacked back into the kitchen. "You want anything to drink?"

"At this hour?"

He pulled a bottle of orange juice from the refrigerator and set it on the breakfast bar. "I was going to drink mine straight, but I could scrounge up some vodka if you prefer yours that way."

I laughed. "Sorry, I misunderstood." *God, what must he think of me?* "I'd love some water. And a couple aspirin. And you wouldn't happen to have an extra toothbrush lying around, would you?"

"Indeed, I do."

He handed me a tall glass of chilled water and I followed him down the hallway, but not the one he'd disappeared down the night before. This hallway was on the opposite side of the living room. He led me past a wall of cabinets to a bathroom with a bedroom directly across from it. From the open doorway I could see the foot of a neatly made bed and a desk with a computer on top.

"Home office," he said, following my gaze, "and guest room. I thought about moving you in there last night, but you seemed content on the couch."

"I still can't believe I fell asleep on you." I was mortified all over again.

"It's all good. I was tired too." Then he opened the cabinet closest to the bathroom and pulled out a toothbrush still in its plastic package and a tube of toothpaste still in the box. "I'll go find you some aspirin," he said and click-clacked down the hall again.

Weird. That was a lot of extra toiletries for a single guy. I wondered if he purposely kept a stock of toothbrushes and toothpaste on hand for women who spent the night. Although, presumably, those other women slept in his bed and not on the couch.

I was still brushing my teeth when he returned with a bottle of acetaminophen, which he placed on the vanity. "I'm going to jump in the shower. Then we can go to breakfast."

I nodded, my mouth still full of minty foam.

Why had I just agreed? I had no desire to go to breakfast with him; I wanted to go home. I could still call an Uber. It wasn't too late. But I couldn't just sneak out while he was in the shower. I'd have to say goodbye first, and then he'd insist on driving me home, and then we'd be right back where we were last night.

I spit out my toothpaste and stared at my reflection in the bathroom mirror. Other than the big black smudges of mascara under my eyes, my face didn't look too terrible. My hair was another matter, but I could pull it back in a ponytail. What I really needed was a shower.

I pulled open the glass door and peeked inside the walk-in shower. There was no soap or shampoo but maybe he had extras of those in the hall closet too, along with some towels.

You could always shower with him.

I actually laughed out loud. *Are you out of your mind?*

It would make breakfast a lot less awkward if you got the s-e-x part out of the way first. Otherwise, you'll be sitting there worrying about it the whole time.

Hmmm. Maybe not the worst idea I'd ever had.

I could hear the water running when I knocked on his closed bathroom door.

"Grace?" he called out.

The floor creaked as I slipped inside the steam-filled bathroom.

Daniel stuck his head out the side of the gray and white striped shower curtain. His hair was wet, but it wasn't filled with suds, so either he hadn't shampooed yet or he'd already rinsed. "What are you doing? Is something wrong?"

"No, I just thought you might like some company."

"Company?"

Oh god, this was a mistake.

Chapter 7

I TURNED AWAY from him and headed to the bathroom door. "Actually, I'm calling an Uber. I just wanted to say goodbye first, so you didn't wonder what happened to me."

"No, don't go," he yelled and shut the water. Then he reached his arm outside the shower curtain and grabbed the towel from the rod. He emerged from the shower-tub combo seconds later dripping water with the fluffy white towel wrapped around his waist. "You startled me, that's all. I'd love to take a shower with you."

"But you already shut off the water." It was all I could think of to say.

"Then I'll turn it back on." Daniel reached inside the shower and turned the knobs. The water immediately started gushing out of the showerhead again.

But he forgot to close the shower curtain and a puddle started forming beside him. "You're getting the floor all wet."

He turned around and pulled the shower curtain, so it was flush with the wall. "Anything else?"

I stared at his taut, glistening body and my heart started to race. I closed the lid on the toilet and sat down. I wanted to blame my lightheadedness on the steamy room, but I knew that wasn't it. "I'm not sure I can do this," I whispered as much to myself as to him.

"Now you don't want to take a shower?" He didn't sound angry, just confused.

I dropped my head in my hands and sighed. "You must think I'm a lunatic."

"No, not at all," he said, but his tone was unconvincing.

"I'm not. Usually." At a minimum he deserved an explanation. "I told you last night I haven't slept with anyone since my husband died."

"I remember."

"Well, I haven't slept with anyone besides my husband in a really long time. The thought of being with someone new is... daunting." Terrifying would be more accurate.

He cracked a smile and kneeled down on the bathroom rug in front of me. "I dated someone for five years before I moved back to Santa Veneta. The first time with a new woman was weird for me too. Although maybe not as weird as this."

I let out a nervous laugh. "Nothing could possibly be as weird as this never-ending first date."

"Technically, I think we're on our second date. To my mind, the first one ended when you started snoring last night."

"God no." I covered my face with my hands. How much worse was this going to get?

"They were very ladylike snores. Totally adorable." He pulled my hands from my face. "I hope to hear more of them."

"Sure you do," I said sarcastically.

"I really do," he said and lightly kissed my lips. "Now let's get you out of these clothes before I run out of hot water."

He lifted my shirt over my head, and I undid my jeans. When I was down to my bra and underwear I turned my back to him, quickly peeled them off and jumped into the shower.

I was still adjusting the water temperature when he stepped in on the far end of the tub. I stayed facing the showerhead, so he only saw me from behind.

"May I wash your hair?" he asked.

"Um, sure. If you want to." Another question no one had ever asked me before, not that I'd ever showered with anyone other than Jonah.

He reached over my shoulder and pulled the shampoo bottle from the shower caddy. "Lean your head back."

I doused my head under the water first then did as he asked, and he began massaging shampoo into my scalp. I don't know how long the scalp massage continued but I was in no hurry for it to end. When he started moving his thumbs in small circles at the base of my skull, I moaned involuntarily. "You could do this for a living."

He chuckled. "I used to."

"Seriously?"

"Didn't I tell you my mom was a hairdresser?"

"No." He hadn't told me anything about his parents other than they'd retired and moved to Arizona, and I hadn't asked.

"She owned a salon on Main near Fifth. I used to work there on the weekends when I was in high school. I started off sweeping floors and washing towels and later she promoted me to shampoo boy."

He moved his thumbs from the base of my skull to behind my ears while the rest of his fingers pushed down on the top of my scalp. I'd never had a shampoo this good before, not even at the expensive salon in Beverly Hills I used to go to when I'd lived in LA. "You must've been very popular."

"I was. The tips were great. That's how I bought my first car. Some of the ladies would only make appointments for the days they knew I worked."

"I would've only made an appointment for the days you worked too."

Eventually, Daniel took his fingers off my scalp and gently turned me around, so I was now facing him instead of the showerhead. "Time to rinse."

"Do we have to?"

"I'm afraid so. But we can condition if you'd like."

I agreed, but he only rubbed the conditioner into my ends.

"It's best to let it soak in for a few minutes then rinse."

I nodded and reached for the bar of soap.

He held out his hand. "May I?" He sensed my hesitation, which I admit was silly since I was standing naked in his shower. "It'll be even better than the shampoo."

"Nothing could be better than that shampoo."

"Try me," he said.

I handed him the bar of soap.

"*Gracias*," he replied and turned me by the shoulders, so I was facing the showerhead again. He started soaping at the back of my neck and worked his way down to my ankles. I assumed at that point he'd want me to face him since he'd only washed the back of me but when I started to turn, he said, "No, you're fine the way you are."

This time he started at the bottom and worked his way up. When he reached my thighs, he stood up and leaned against me as he continued to soap my midsection, my breasts, which he spent an inordinate amount of time washing, then my shoulders and neck. The one area he had avoided was my vagina.

He leaned his chin on my shoulder and whispered into my ear. "You okay?"

"Yes," I said. "But no offense, the shampoo was better."

He laughed. "We're not done yet!" He rubbed the soap in his hands until they were filled with suds then placed the bar back in the soap dish. He reached around me and placed his soapy hands on the inside of my thighs and began rhythmically stroking my legs, moving closer and closer to my vagina.

I was tingling all over when I asked, "Do you have a—"

"Shhh," he said, anticipating my question. "Not yet."

It was his fingers that brought me to a shuddering orgasm. I moaned so loud I told him I hoped his neighbors weren't home. Daniel just laughed.

I stepped out of the tub first and picked up the towel he'd left on the floor.

"Let me get you a clean one," Daniel said, slipping out of the bathroom and returning with two more fluffy white towels. I dropped the wet towel I'd been using onto the bathtub and wrapped the dry one around myself. He wrapped his towel around his shoulders instead of his waist. I couldn't help but look, and I was not disappointed with the view.

"Would you like some help with that?" I asked.

He glanced down at his erection then smiled up at me. "What did you have in mind?"

"What do you like?" I asked, hoping he wasn't going to suggest something I'd never tried before.

"I'd like to be inside you."

"I think that can be arranged."

Chapter 8

We never made it to a restaurant for breakfast. Instead, Daniel toasted two bagels, which we ate together in bed. I'd thought my bed was comfortable, but his had mine beat. I felt like I was lying in a high-end hotel bed—firm but with lots of cushioning and super soft sheets.

"Be careful," I said when he brought me a second cup of coffee with the milk and sugar already stirred in. "I could get used to this."

He smiled. "That's the idea."

"So, this was all part of your master plan?"

He set his coffee cup down on the nightstand and joined me under the duvet. "No, I thought you'd want to take things slow."

"Because I'm a nice girl?" I giggled. Did men still think that way?

"No, because of your husband."

I froze. I hadn't thought of Jonah since last night. But now he was suddenly in the forefront of my mind and a wave of grief washed over me.

"Uh oh," Daniel said. "I said the wrong thing, didn't I?"

"No, it's fine," I said, pulling the duvet up to my chin.

"You mentioned him earlier, so I thought it was okay. I don't know what the rules are. I've never been in this situation before."

"Me either."

"So, we're both virgins."

"Except for the fact that I actually gave birth to a child."

That killed the mood. Daniel rolled over onto his back putting a space between us.

"Sorry," I said.

"You don't need to apologize."

Maybe not, but my comment hung in the air between us. "I should go."

Daniel rolled onto his side and reached for my hand. "I don't want you to go. I just want you to give me some ground rules."

"Ground rules?"

"Guidance. So I know what not to say. I don't want to keep upsetting you."

He was the one who was upset, not me. But his request was not unreasonable. I just didn't think it was one I could fulfill. "There are no rules, Daniel. The grief just comes on like that sometimes. Suddenly and without warning. One minute I'm fine and the next I'm in tears. My therapist says it's normal."

"You have a therapist?"

I nodded. I almost said it was one of the conditions of my release from the Wellstone Center, but I caught myself in time.

"And that helps?" he asked.

"Some." It didn't lessen the grief any, but it gave it context and made me feel normal again.

"I'm glad."

We laid together in silence while I wondered how much longer I needed to stay before I could get up and leave without him getting upset with me again.

Then he said, "I hope this isn't the last time I'm ever going to see you."

He sounded sincere and that surprised me. I couldn't imagine Daniel had a hard time finding women to date. In my Before life he would've checked off all the boxes on my list. But in my After life, I no longer had a list. I wasn't even sure I was ready to start dating again, and I certainly wasn't ready for a serious relationship. The best part of our date had been the sex. But if that's all he wanted from me, then maybe this could work. "It won't be if you don't want it to be," I said.

"I don't want to keep upsetting you."

"*You* didn't upset me. I just get upset sometimes. And that's not going to change no matter how much therapy I have."

"Then I don't want to keep saying the wrong thing."

"You didn't. There is no wrong thing. And no right thing." But I could tell from the sour expression on his face he wasn't satisfied with my answer. I sighed. If I wanted to have sex with him again, and I did, then I'd have to give him what he wanted from me. "Okay, ground rules. Don't raise the topic with me, but I might sometimes raise it with you. I can't pretend my husband and child never existed, but I don't want to talk about them all the time either. I'm trying to live in the present, not the past, but sometimes the past intrudes on the present and there's nothing I can do about it. If this is going to work, you have to be okay with that."

"I'm okay with it."

"Then we're good." I smiled.

In response his penis stood straight up, pitching a tent in the sheets. We both laughed.

Daniel said, "He knows there's a beautiful woman in his bed."

"I'm sure I'm not the first."

"No," Daniel admitted. "But maybe the last."

The only reason I wasn't terrified was because I knew he was feeding me a line.

WHEN I TOLD Daniel I had to leave because I was going to a barbecue that afternoon, he offered to accompany me, but I declined. This date had already lasted much longer than it should have. Plus, I knew if I showed up at Tim and Richard's house with Daniel on my arm, Tim would immediately start planning our wedding.

I parked on the street in front of Tim and Richard's house and let myself into their backyard through the side gate. I'd assumed everyone would be gathered on the patio as usual, but it was empty. Richard hadn't even turned on the grill yet. I walked to the back door and peeked in through the glass window, but all I could see was the laundry piled on top of the washing machine. I returned to the front of the house. Both cars were parked in the driveway, so I knew they were home.

I knocked on the front door. As soon as Jayden opened it, I could hear Tim and Richard's raised voices from upstairs. Jayden didn't stick around to explain. He disappeared into the back of the house, where I assumed the rest of the kids were hiding too. I was debating between going to check on them or turning around and leaving, when Richard bolted down the steps. He stopped short when he saw me. "Grace, I didn't know you were here."

"I just got here. I thought we were barbecuing this afternoon." I set the box of cupcakes I'd purchased on the way over on the console table. "I must've gotten my dates mixed up. Sorry."

"No, we just lost track of time," Richard said, "Come in."

"No, I'll leave. Or I can take the kids for a while if you guys need some time alone." I didn't know how I'd fit six children in my car, but we'd figure it out. Or we could always go for a walk in the neighborhood.

Tim appeared at the top of the staircase. He looked upset, but when he saw me, he pasted a smile on his face and said, "Don't go. We're celebrating."

"You are?"

"Yes," he said, joining Richard at the bottom of the stairs. "We're getting a baby!"

Chapter 9

"Congratulations!" I shouted. I looked from Tim to Richard and back to Tim. Neither looked happy about the news. "That's what you wanted, isn't it?"

"Yes," Richard replied then paused before adding, "Maybe not at this precise moment in time though."

"No time like the present," Tim said.

Richard glared at him.

"This seems like something you two should celebrate alone," I said. "Are you sure you don't want me to take the kids for a few hours? I don't mind, but I may need to borrow your minivan."

"Don't be ridiculous," Tim said. Then he noticed the bakery box sitting on the console table. "You brought cupcakes. It's a party."

Richard went outside to light the grill, and the kids slowly trickled out of their hiding spaces. Tim shooed them all out to the backyard along with the dogs. The cat and the gecko remained hidden somewhere inside the house.

Tim pulled a package of ground beef out of the refrigerator and started dividing it up into similarly sized balls. At his direction I chopped tomatoes and cucumbers for a salad.

I waited until we'd both gotten into a rhythm before I said, "I don't want to pry but—"

Tim smacked a ball of ground beef, flattening it into a patty. "I love him, Grace. But sometimes he is just impossible, especially about money."

I'd had my fair share of money arguments with Jonah too. We just had different priorities. Jonah claimed it was because I grew up wanting for almost nothing, while he grew up wanting for almost everything.

According to the magazine article I'd read in Dr. Rubenstein's waiting room last week, the number one issue couples fight about is money. Sex and children are numbers two and three.

Although Tim and Richard's house was large, I knew they hadn't purchased it. Richard told me he'd inherited the house from his mother when she died. Other than the money they received from the State for fostering, they were a one-income family. Tim previously worked as a graphic designer, but these days his job was to take care of the house and the kids. Richard was a physician's assistant in a doctor's office, but I had no idea how much that paid.

"He's probably just worried," I said. "When I was pregnant with Amelia, Jonah was a stressed out mess. We argued all the time. But after Amelia was born, he was fine."

"I know he's nervous," Tim replied. "I am too. The agency called us this morning and told us we need to pick up the baby from the hospital tomorrow."

"Wow, they don't give you much notice." At least Jonah and I had nine months to prepare.

"No," Tim said, pounding out another patty. "If I had more time, then I could've gotten us everything we needed used. But with one day's notice, I have to buy new. What choice do I have?"

"You could shop at Ikea," Richard said. I spun around and found him standing in the entrance to the kitchen. I hadn't heard him come inside. I thought he was still in the backyard with the kids. "It doesn't have to be Pottery Barn," Richard continued.

"You want your son to sleep in a crib made of sawdust?" Tim asked.

"It's not sawdust," Richard replied. "It's particleboard. And the Pottery Barn crib wasn't solid wood either."

"Just so you know," I said, keeping my eyes focused on the cucumber I was slicing, "the baby's not going to sleep in the crib for the first few months anyway. Most people start with a bassinet in their bedroom then move the baby to a crib when they're older."

"See," Richard said. "We don't even need a crib yet. Let me ask around at work. Maybe someone has a crib they're not using anymore."

"I have one," I said.

Both Richard and Tim stared at me.

"I've got everything—a crib, a dresser, a changing table, the bassinet too. Nice stuff," I said to Tim. "You'll like it. Although you'll probably want to buy new bedding because mine's all pink."

"You still have Amelia's things?" Tim asked.

"Everything but her clothes, although you wouldn't want them anyway. They definitely looked like girl clothes. But I still have all the furniture." I could feel the tears welling in my eyes, but I didn't let them escape.

Richard glanced at Tim, then back at me. "No, Grace. We can't ask you to do that."

"You didn't ask. I offered." I sniffed back my tears and forced a smile. "And you would be doing me a favor. My mother's been hounding me to get rid of this stuff since the day after the funeral. She'll probably send you a thank-you card."

Tim wiped his hands on a dish towel and hugged me. "I'm sure when you're ready you will," he said, "but not today. Not for us."

He let go of me and I stepped back and wiped my eyes. "Please let me do this. Otherwise, I'll just end up donating it all to some random charity, and I'd much rather it went to people who I know will give it a good home."

Tim and Richard exchanged another glance.

"Are you sure?" Richard asked. "Absolutely sure?"

"We don't want to pressure you," Tim added.

"You're not pressuring me. I offered. You'll be doing me a favor by taking it off my hands."

Chapter 10

"You WANT SOME COFFEE?" I asked Richard when he arrived at my house early the next morning. He had dark circles under his eyes, and I wondered if he'd slept at all last night.

"No, it'll just make me more jittery. Do you have a toolbox? I left mine sitting next to the front door so I wouldn't forget, and I still walked out of the house without it."

"Sure," I said. "I'll go get it."

When I returned with the toolbox Richard took it from me and followed me up the steps. When I opened the door to Amelia's room, his jaw dropped. I didn't know if his reaction was because he liked the décor or because the room still looked exactly like it had when Amelia was alive. Other than packing up her clothes and diapers, I hadn't changed anything.

"You're sure you want to do this?" Richard asked as I pulled the bassinet out of the closet where my mother had hidden it away after the funeral.

"Yes," I said without hesitation. It was time.

"What about these?" Richard nodded to the dresser where the books, nightlight, and the few items of clothing I intended to save were still sitting, along with Jonah's flash drive. I'd stashed the flash drive in Amelia's room a few weeks ago to stop myself from obsessively checking it every day. *Out of sight, out of mind*, I'd told myself, which wasn't true. I still thought about it all the time, I just no longer plugged it into my computer daily trying to guess the password.

"You're welcome to the nightlight," I said. "I'm keeping the rest."

Richard handed me the flash drive first. "Baby photos?" he asked. "Or was Amelia so advanced you were already teaching her coding?"

I laughed. "I actually have no idea what's on it. You wouldn't know how to circumvent a password on one of these, would you?"

"Sorry," he said. "I can barely remember my own. I know they tell you not to write them down, but I have to. I forgot my bank password once and it was a bitch getting access again."

"I know. I always write them down too. But apparently my husband didn't."

At the mention of Jonah, Richard looked away. I was used to that reaction and didn't take offense.

Richard decided to disassemble the changing table first. I sat down on the floor next to him and handed him tools. "You'll never guess where I found the flash drive," I said to distract myself from the sadness I could feel overtaking me.

"Where?" he asked, removing the bottom shelf.

"In here," I said, holding up the empty diaper caddy. He looked at it quizzically. "It's for diapers. It attaches to the side of the table. That way you can hold onto the baby with one hand while you reach for a clean diaper with the other."

"I guess that makes sense."

"It'll make a lot more sense when you change your first diaper."

Richard laughed. "I'm sure it will."

Neither one of us spoke as he unscrewed the second shelf and placed it on the floor on top of the first. Then he turned to me. "Isn't a diaper bin kind of an odd place to store a flash drive?"

Chapter 11

"THANK YOU!" I shouted, and Richard leaned away from me, startled by my sudden outburst. "Sorry. It's just nice to have someone agree with me for a change."

"You mean no one else thinks it's odd? Storing flash drives with diapers is common?"

I stared at Richard. This was my chance to get an objective opinion. I really wanted one, especially from a man.

"Let me get this straight," Richard said. He was sitting on the floor with his back against the wall, his hands wrapped around a coffee cup, all the pieces of what had once been Amelia's changing table stacked in a neat pile next to him. "Your husband bought a five-million-dollar life insurance policy and he never told you?"

"Not only did he not tell me," I said, "he hid it in our safe deposit box behind the one-million-dollar policy I did know about."

"So you'd likely never find it unless he died."

"Exactly," I said. "Now isn't that suspicious?"

"I don't know if it's suspicious, but it does seem odd."

"It's more than just odd when you combine it with all the

other facts." I started counting them off on my fingers. "The key he gave his brother, Jake sneaking into the house and refusing to tell me why, the flash drive. All circumstantial evidence, sure, but that's what cases are built on."

"And what case are you building?" he asked.

The million-dollar question.

Richard glanced down at his watch. "Oh shit. I'm going to be late for work." He set his coffee cup down on the dresser and started snatching up the pieces of the changing table. "Do you have something I could put these in?"

"Leave it," I said. "I'll drive it over to your house later with the bassinet."

"Are you sure?" he asked, but he was already setting the pieces on the floor again.

"Yes. Go to work. You have a baby to support!" It would also give me an opportunity to stop at the store first and buy them a gift.

I ARRIVED at Tim and Richard's house later that morning with the bassinet, a shopping bag filled with all the pieces of the changing table, and an infant car seat, my gift to them. I would've stayed and helped Tim install the car seat, but I had a court appearance in half an hour, and I couldn't be late.

After my hearing I drove to the office, but I couldn't concentrate. All I could think about was the flash drive. I finally gave up on work and went home. I retrieved the flash drive from Amelia's room, plugged it into my laptop, and started guessing. I was no more successful this time than I had been all the other times before.

I was still typing in random numbers, letters, and special characters when Daniel called.

"How was your day?" he asked.

"Okay," I said, then pulled the flash drive out of my computer and threw it across the room. It bounced off the closet door and landed on the rug. "Yours?"

"Great," he replied. "Hey, do you like Peruvian food?"

"I don't think I know what Peruvian food is," I answered as I retrieved the flash drive and plugged it back into my computer. Thankfully, I hadn't damaged it. The password prompt popped up on the screen and I sighed.

"The most well-known dish is ceviche, but there are many others."

"I didn't know ceviche was Peruvian. I thought it was Spanish." I typed ceviche into the password box and, unsurprisingly, it spit back the same password incorrect message it had given me thousands of times before.

Daniel kept talking but I stopped listening until I heard him shout, "Hello? Grace, are you there?"

I hit enter on my latest password attempt and was greeted with the same error message. "Yeah. Sorry, I got distracted."

"I asked if you wanted to come over tonight. I'll cook you my Peruvian roast chicken. It's my mother's recipe. Or something else if you prefer."

"Actually, I think I'll take a raincheck if you don't mind." I typed in a combination of my and Amelia's birthdates, which I knew I'd tried before, but this time I added random characters at the end. Fail.

"Oh. Okay. Is another night this week better for you?"

"I'm not sure. I'm kind of in the middle of something right now." This time I typed in our birthdates in reverse with an exclamation point at the end. That failed too. There had to be a better way.

"In the middle of something. Is that your way of telling me you don't want to see me again?"

"No, I'm just busy that's all."

"Too busy to get together tonight or any other night this week?"

I sighed. "Daniel, this has nothing to do with you."

"Right. It's not you, it's me. I think I've used that line myself before, so I guess I deserve this."

"It's not what you think."

"I think I had a great time with you this weekend. I thought you had a great time with me too. But I guess I was wrong."

"No, I did have a great time." I hadn't realized how much I missed sex until I started having it again.

"Then what's the problem, Grace?"

"Nothing. I just can't deal with this right now."

"Okay, let me know when you can *deal with this*," he said before he hung up on me.

Goddamnit!

I BUZZED Daniel's apartment from the call box outside the entrance to his building.

When his voice came through the intercom I said, "It's me and I brought chicken. I don't think it's Peruvian, but it smells good."

"Did you bring wine?" he asked.

"No, but I can go out and get some if you tell me what you want."

"I'll open a bottle," he said and buzzed me in.

He was waiting for me at the entrance to his apartment wearing sweatpants and a Cal Berkley T-shirt with a hole in it. "Sorry about the attire. I wasn't expecting company."

"No problem." I'd changed into yoga pants and a T-shirt when I'd gotten home from work, and I hadn't bothered to change back into something nicer before I came over. I figured after we ate dinner, we'd be getting naked so it didn't really matter what I wore.

Daniel took the white plastic bag from my hand and gave me a peck on the lips. "Thanks for coming tonight."

"I didn't want you to think I was blowing you off because I wasn't. I'm just really mad at my husband right now."

Daniel froze.

"It's okay. I brought him up, so you're allowed to talk about him."

"Um, okay," he said cautiously then locked the front door.

"Mad's not the right word," I said, setting my purse down on the breakfast bar. "Frustrated is more accurate, and maybe a little angry too."

"Angry?"

I pulled the flash drive out of the zippered compartment of my purse and held it out to him. "You don't happen to know how to hack into one of these, do you?"

Unfortunately, Daniel did not know how to hack into a flash drive. But he did spend some time after dinner trying to unlock it on his computer.

"And you have no idea what's on it?" he asked again, clicking various boxes and dropdown menus.

"None. I can't even say for certain it was my husband's." That was the latest theory I'd come up with while I was waiting in line at the chicken place. Maybe the flash drive actually belonged to Jake, not Jonah, and he'd hidden it in our house. Or Jonah hid it for him. That made more sense and would also explain why Jonah gave him a key. But wouldn't he have told Jake where he'd hidden it? And it still didn't explain the life insurance policy.

Daniel stopped clicking and turned to face me. "If it's not your husband's and it's not yours, then whose is it?"

"I have no idea." There was no way I was telling Daniel my latest theory. He probably already thought I was borderline psycho from my behavior this weekend. I didn't want him to think I was completely insane. Plus, I had no proof it was Jake's flash drive. I wouldn't know whose it was until I could unlock it.

"Well, who else has access to your house?"

"My mom and my aunt," I said, "but it's not theirs either."

"So if it's not theirs, and it's not yours, then that just leaves your husband, right?"

"Right," I said and looked away.

Daniel turned his attention back to his computer. "Did your husband ever work from home?"

"Sometimes," I said. "Why?"

"Maybe this is a work flash drive. It would explain the password. Didn't you say he was a money manager?"

"Accountant. But he worked for a money management firm."

"I'm sure his firm would require all financial files be password protected."

That was a good point. I was imagining something nefarious when there could be an innocent explanation. Except... "Why hide it in our daughter's bedroom?"

"Are you sure he hid it there? Maybe he just dropped it or it fell out of his pocket."

"I'm sure. My aunt found it taped to the bottom of the diaper caddy."

Daniel looked at me blankly.

"It's the thing where you stack the clean diapers."

Daniel shrugged. "I once lost a flash drive in the garbage. It must've fallen out of my pocket when I was closing the bag. Fishing it out of the dumpster was not fun."

"But you found it *in* the dumpster not taped to the bottom."

"True," he said. "My point was things do go lost sometimes. Especially small things." He pulled the flash drive out of his computer and handed it to me. "If I were you, I'd call the IT person at your husband's firm and ask them if they have the recovery key."

"What's a recovery key?"

"Depending on which program your husband used to encrypt the drive, he would've received a recovery key to use in case he ever forgot the password."

"And that's something the IT person would have? Because a couple of weeks after Jonah died, they sent someone over to the house to pick up his laptop."

"The recovery key isn't something that would've been stored on his hard drive. The IT department keeps a master list of all the recovery keys in a secure file. Or at least that's how we did it at my old company."

"Okay, I'll call tomorrow. Thanks for your help with this."

"Anytime. And if you need help with anything else, say washing your hair..."

I laughed. "Actually, I do need to wash my hair." I'd intended to shower after Richard left this morning, but then I'd gotten distracted with the flash drive.

"I can help with that too."

Chapter 12

I CALLED Jonah's office the next morning as I drove from Daniel's house back to my own. It was still so early I wasn't surprised when no one picked up and my call went directly to a prerecorded message. I followed the phone tree prompts until I reached the voicemail for Jonah's former assistant. I left her an anodyne message asking her to call me back. Then I waited. And waited. And waited some more. My heart raced every time the phone rang, but it was never Jonah's assistant. It was a relief to go to my appointment with Dr. Rubenstein that afternoon. It meant I could silence my phone for an hour and not have to think about it.

"HOW WAS YOUR VACATION?" I asked Dr. Rubenstein as soon as we'd both settled into our usual spots in her office—her on her Eames chair and me on the corner of the green chenille couch. The skin on her chest and arms was tanner than usual and provided an even more striking contrast to her silver hair.

"Very relaxing," she said. "How are you doing?"

"Good. You missed a lot."

Then I proceeded to fill her in on meeting Maria, sleeping with Daniel, and giving away Amelia's furniture. I also told her about Daniel's suggestion to call Jonah's office for the recovery key to the flash drive, but she wasn't interested in that. All she wanted to talk about was Daniel and how giving away Amelia's furniture made me feel.

I turned my phone on as I walked back to my car and saw I had a voicemail from Jonah's office. I didn't even listen to the message. I just hit the call back button and waited until a familiar voice came on the line.

"Hi, Kristie, it's Grace Hughes."

"Mrs. Hughes, it was so nice to hear from you again. How are you?"

"Well. And you?"

"Oh, you know me. Just trying to stay out of trouble."

Kristie did have a knack for saying the wrong thing, to the wrong person, at the wrong time. When I'd called this morning, I wasn't even sure she'd still be working at the firm. It would not have surprised me to learn she'd been fired.

"Funny you called today," she continued. "I was just thinking about Jonah."

"Really? Why?"

"We had a meeting this morning and the partners asked me to start planning this year's holiday party. I was thinking of going with the movie theme again."

I remembered the last movie-themed holiday party. Jonah had just joined the firm and felt uncomfortable dressing up as his favorite character—Batman—so we decided he should wear a tuxedo and tell everyone he was James Bond. For the record, Jonah did not look like any of the actors who played 007. I donned a blond wig and a pink suit and went as the lawyer from *Legally Blonde*. For the record, I don't look like Reese Witherspoon either.

"And that made you think of Jonah?" I asked.

"Sure. Don't you remember the belly dancer? I think she was Matt's date."

I remembered Matt's date, even though I'd only met her that one time.

"I still have the video of her giving Jonah a lap dance!" Kristie continued.

I did not have the video, but I didn't need it. I vividly remembered the lap dance. Or I vividly remembered the huge fight Jonah and I had about it when we'd gotten home that night. Jonah had claimed he was just playing along because he was the new guy. I'd told him his story would be more believable had his tongue not been hanging out of his mouth the entire time.

After a pause Kristie said, "Sorry. I probably shouldn't have brought it up. But Jonah was never unfaithful, at least that I know about. And I can't say the same for some of the other guys around here."

I closed my eyes and breathed deeply then exhaled. "Thanks, Kristie, but that's not why I called. Can you please give me the contact info for the firm's IT person?"

"Sure." I could hear her fingernails tapping on a keyboard. "Why do you want to talk to him? Computer problems? Because I don't think he freelances."

"No, I found a flash drive the other day, but I can't open it because I don't know the password. I'm hoping he has the recovery key."

The click-clacking of the keyboard stopped. "You found Jonah's flash drive?"

"Well, I found *a* flash drive. I'm not even a hundred percent sure it's Jonah's. That's why I wanted to talk to IT."

"Is it okay if I put you on hold for a minute?"

The line went silent before I could answer. And the next voice I heard on the phone was not Kristie's.

Chapter 13

"Grace, Brian Sullivan here."

I recognized the booming voice of Jonah's former boss even before he said his name. The last time I'd seen him was at the funeral. I was sure we must've spoken that day, but I had no memory of the conversation. "Hi, Brian. How are you?"

"Terrific. Too much time in restaurants though and not enough time on the links. But you gotta keep the clients happy, right? Those tuition bills don't pay themselves."

Brian's job was to keep the clients happy. Jonah's job had been to reduce their tax burden, or as I called it, legal tax evasion. Jonah insisted he followed all IRS regulations. I knew that was true, but as I used to tell Jonah, just because it's legal, doesn't mean it's right.

"Kristie told me you found Jonah's flash drive," Brian continued.

"I told her I found *a* flash drive. I didn't realize one was missing."

"Not missing. We just discovered some irregularities after Jonah passed, that's all. So we've been looking through some of his files."

I could practically see Brian Sullivan sitting in his corner office, leaning back in his big leather chair with his feet up on his desk, his hands folded across his ample stomach, and his dress shirt straining at the buttons. Jonah often complained about the endless hours he'd had to waste sitting in on calls in Brian's office when he could've been back at his desk getting work done.

"What kind of irregularities?" I asked. As far as I knew, the firm had been happy with Jonah's work. He'd received a raise and a bonus the month before he died.

"Nothing for you to worry about," Brian said. "But we do need to see the flash drive. Can you bring it by the office this afternoon? Or if that's not convenient for you, we can send a messenger to your house to pick it up. Are you still at the same address?"

Alarm bells started going off in my head. Something about this wasn't right. He was too eager. "Yes, but I'm not home. I'm at work."

"Do you have the flash drive with you? I can send a messenger to your office right now to pick it up."

"You don't need to go to all that trouble. I'll just bring it by one day next week."

"No trouble at all, Grace. I insist. What's your address?"

I didn't dislike Brian, I just never trusted him. And I trusted him even less now. There was no way I was giving him this flash drive without knowing what was on it. But he wouldn't take no for an answer, so I told him to send a messenger to my office later in the afternoon. And as soon as we hung up, I drove directly to Best Buy. Luckily, they carried the same brand Jonah used.

I brought my newly purchased flash drive to the office and googled instructions for how to add a password. It looked simple enough, but lots of things with technology that were supposed to be simple never seemed to work that easily for me, so I decided to wait for MJ. I ambushed him as soon as he walked through the front door.

"Do you know how to add a password to a flash drive?"

He slipped his backpack off his shoulders and sat down at the reception desk. "No, but I bet I can figure it out."

"Can you figure it out quickly?" Brian's messenger was scheduled to arrive in half an hour.

MJ followed me into my office and plugged the flash drive into my computer.

"What are you putting on here you don't want anyone to see?" he asked as he moved the mouse around the screen with dizzying speed.

"Nothing."

"Then why you adding a password?"

He was right. It would look odd if I sent Brian an empty flash drive. Although without my password, he wouldn't be able to open it, so how would he know? But unlike me, Brian had an IT person and that person might have a way of figuring it out. Even I knew it was possible to check how much memory had been used, even if I didn't know how to check it myself. I tapped the photo app on my phone and turned the screen toward MJ. "Can you transfer these pictures to the flash drive?"

"Sure. Are they saved in the cloud?"

"How would I know?"

MJ rolled his eyes.

"You know I'm bad at this stuff. Here," I said and handed him my phone. "You figure it out."

Half an hour later Brian Sullivan's messenger left my office with a flash drive containing 212 photos mostly of Amelia, but a handful with me and Jonah too. I'd sealed it in an envelope with a note asking Brian to return it to me with the recovery key if he found anything personal on it. I didn't actually care if he returned it. I just figured that's what an innocent person would say.

MJ waited until the messenger had sped away on his motorcycle before he said, "Can I ask why you gave that guy all your photos?"

I pulled Jonah's flash drive out of the zippered compartment of my purse. "No, but can you break the password on this one?"

MJ let out a laugh. "I can fix your printer when it's jammed, but I ain't no hacker."

Normally, I'd be happy to hear MJ wasn't breaking the law, but not today. "Do you know any hackers? Maybe a kid at your school?"

"At the Winston Academy? Are you kidding me?"

This time I was the one who rolled my eyes. His classmates were privileged; that didn't mean they were saints. "Someone at your old school then? I'll pay. I'm not asking anyone to work for free."

"You shoulda said that to begin with." MJ opened his palm, and I placed the flash drive in his hand. He plugged it into my computer and started zooming the mouse around the screen again. "What's on here that's so important?"

"I don't know. That's why I need a hacker. So I can find out."

After ten minutes, MJ ejected the flash drive and handed it back to me. "Sorry, Grace, hacking ain't my thing."

"Any idea where I can find a hacker?" I didn't think they advertised, but maybe they did if you knew where to look.

"No, but my uncle might."

Chapter 14

I DROVE MJ back to Tim and Richard's house. Usually I just dropped him off, but today I parked and went inside because I wanted to meet baby Aaron. He was adorable. Pudgy with light brown skin and a scalp full of fuzzy black hair. The last baby I'd held in my arms was Amelia. I was afraid holding Aaron would trigger me, but it didn't. Maybe if he'd been a pink-cheeked girl with a smattering of dark blonde hair, I would've gotten upset, but holding this tiny brown boy just made me smile.

I stayed long enough to watch Tim feed Aaron, change him, and rock him to sleep. Then I drove home and called MJ's uncle.

Alex picked up on the second ring. "Yo, counselor."

He must've had my number programmed into his phone. It had been months since we'd spoken. "Hi, Alex. How are you?"

"Can't complain. Everything okay? Kids alright?"

"Yeah, I just dropped MJ off at home. Have you met his dads yet?"

"Nope."

"You should. They're really nice people."

"Is that why you called? To tell me I need to meet the *gay* guys raising my niece and nephew?"

I gritted my teeth. "You should be thanking those gay guys. If it wasn't for them, god knows where MJ and Sofia would've ended up."

"They could've just stayed with you and your aunt."

"You know if it was up to me, they would have." He'd been at my aunt's house the day she decided to give them up.

"But you had to follow the law."

"Yes, Alex, I'm a lawyer. That's what lawyers do. And if you were a law-abiding citizen, they could be living with you."

"Are you accusing me of something?"

"No." It was my office landlord, Mike Murphy, who'd told me Alex was a big-time drug dealer in LA. But I'd never asked Alex, mainly because I didn't want to know.

After an uncomfortable silence, he said, "So what do you want? You didn't call just to say hi."

"No," I admitted. "MJ thought you might be able to help me with something."

"Help with what?"

"I need to hire a hacker."

"Sorry, counselor, not my area. And for a smart lady, you're pretty fucking stupid sometimes." Then the line went dead.

A minute later I received a text from an unknown number. *Not a conversation you have over the phone. Saturday@2. Your house.*

"I still don't understand why you switched out the flash drives," Daniel said.

We were having dinner at his apartment—sushi and Japanese lager, presumably with sex to follow. At least, I hoped there would be sex to follow since it was the only reason I'd agreed to come to his house again tonight.

I dipped the edge of my California roll into the wasabi sauce. I was just starting to eat spicy food again. After Jonah and Amelia died, I ate only bland food, if I ate at all. "I told you. He spooked me."

"I don't know what that means," Daniel said, dunking his sashimi into the wasabi before popping it into his mouth whole.

"It means I don't trust Brian Sullivan. Why was he in such a hurry to get his hands on the flash drive?"

Daniel washed down his mouthful of sushi with a swallow of beer. "Because he's been looking for it all this time?"

I shook my head. "Nope. Not buying it. If he'd been looking for the flash drive all this time, then why didn't he ever call me and ask me if I had it?"

"Maybe he didn't want to disturb you because he knew you were grieving."

"Not a chance." Caring about other people's feelings was not Brian's M.O. "He had no problem sending someone to my house to pick up Jonah's laptop a couple of weeks after he died. And I actually was grieving then."

Daniel shrugged and popped another piece of sashimi into his mouth. After he chewed and swallowed, he said, "I can practically see the wheels turning in your head."

He was right. My brain was spinning. I felt like I was trapped in a maze trying to find my way out. "They've had Jonah's laptop almost this entire time. If files were missing and Jonah had them, isn't that where they'd be?"

"If they took the laptop back to give to another employee, then I'm sure they would've wiped the hard drive first. That's standard procedure."

"But wouldn't they have checked the hard drive before they wiped it?"

"Checked it for what? If they didn't know anything was missing, then they wouldn't have known to look."

"Exactly!"

Daniel stared at me blankly.

"You just said it made sense for Brian to be in a rush to get the flash drive because he'd been looking for these missing files the whole time. Now you're saying he didn't know they were missing until recently. Which is it, Daniel? It can't be both."

"Whoa." He held his hands up. "Back down. I don't have a dog in this fight."

"Well, I do. My family was murdered. I need to know why."

"You already do. Some crazy guy shot them."

I stared down at my plate.

"Well, that's what happened, isn't it?"

"Yes." That's what the police told me at the time, and I had no reason not to believe them. Yet I couldn't shake the feeling there was more—and the flash drive was the key.

Chapter 15

I WAS PACING my living room at 2:23 p.m. on Saturday when Alex's black BMW pulled up in front of my house. I opened my front door while he was still walking up the flagstone path. "I was starting to wonder if that text was really from you."

Alex was wearing his usual black jeans, black T-shirt, and black leather jacket, despite it being sunny and seventy-eight degrees outside. Someday I wanted to peek in his closet to see if he even owned any clothing in another color. "I took the kids to see Maria. They wanted to stop for lunch on the way back."

"How's she doing?" I said, shutting the door behind him.

"Okay," he said as he glanced around. "For now."

"Did they say how long she'd be there?" I'd asked Dr. Simpson last week but she'd said she couldn't disclose any information to me because I wasn't a family member. But when I'd asked MJ, he didn't know either.

"No, but I'm sure they'll get rid of her as soon as possible. They don't like to keep the poor people any longer than they have to."

I wanted to object but assumed he was right. I doubted the government paid the Wellstone Center as much as private insurance companies did, so naturally they'd want to release those patients as soon as it was legal for them to do so.

"Where will she live when she gets out?" I knew she couldn't go back to her apartment because she'd been evicted. Her belongings were still sitting in two garbage bags inside my aunt's garage.

He shrugged.

"What about MJ and Sofia? They can't move back in with her if she doesn't have a place to live."

"You tell me, counselor."

I was still new to practicing family law. I'd been working with Janelle for several months but, so far, she'd only handed me the minor's counsel cases, which meant upper income kids. The children I represented may have been emotionally abandoned by their parents, but they all had a place to sleep.

"I'll ask Janelle. You want something to drink? Coffee? Tea? Water?"

"Coffee. Black."

"I remember."

Alex smiled, apparently recalling our first meeting at Starbucks too. It was only six months ago but felt like another lifetime.

I headed into the kitchen, but Alex didn't follow. He lingered in the hallway. The Keurig had just finished spitting out the second cup of coffee when Alex appeared holding the framed wedding photo that usually hung on my wall.

"One of these your husband?" Alex asked. It was a picture of me, Jonah, and Jake. I was in the center with the men on either side.

"Yes. My husband's the one on the left wearing the silver cummerbund and tie." Jake's cummerbund and tie were black.

He nodded and returned the photograph to its spot on the wall.

I handed Alex his coffee and he followed me into the living room. I settled onto the couch and Alex sat down on the chair across from me.

"Nice house," he said, glancing around the room.

I was surprised he hadn't commented on the size of the television since everyone else did. Maybe he had a giant TV of his own. "Thanks," I said. "I assume MJ filled you in." And had given him my home address since Alex hadn't asked me for it, although I supposed he could've found it online.

"All he told me was you were looking for someone to hack a flash drive."

"Yes. I can't open it without the password, which I don't have, nor do I have the recovery key. Do you know anyone who could hack into it for me?"

He held the coffee mug in both hands and looked at me. "Is it yours?"

I wasn't expecting that question, although maybe I should have. "Does it matter?"

"It might."

I paused then said, "It was found in my house."

"Not the same thing."

We stared at each other across the coffee table. I really didn't want to divulge any information to Alex. But I needed his help. And he didn't seem inclined to help me if I didn't explain. But attorney-client privilege doesn't apply when the attorney is the one breaking the law.

"I'm not asking you to do anything illegal," I said.

"You're asking me to help you find someone to hack a flash drive."

"Yes, but it's not illegal if it's my flash drive. It's like breaking into your own house. That's not a crime."

"Is it your flash drive?" he asked again.

I sighed. "It was my husband's, and I was his sole beneficiary. So that makes it mine now." That wasn't one hundred percent true. If the flash drive was the property of Jonah's employer, then Jonah's employer still owned it. But since becoming a lawyer, I'd learned if you say something with authority people tend to believe you. Alex seemed to.

"What's on it?" he asked.

"Well, if I knew that I wouldn't need someone to hack into it for me, now would I?"

"What do you *think* is on it?"

"Honestly, I have no idea. Why all the questions? Either you know someone or you don't."

"I might. But I need to know what I'm dealing with." He set his mug down on the coffee table and leaned forward. Then he lowered his voice as if he was afraid we'd be overheard, even though we were the only two people in the house. "I don't want to put you in danger."

I sealed my lips together to stifle a laugh. Alex could be so dramatic sometimes. I lowered my voice too and said, "How could hacking my own flash drive put me in danger? I was planning on paying the guy. No one's going to have to break my legs."

He bit his lip and stared down at his hands.

"Why are you being so weird about this? No one's going to care that I hired a hacker."

He looked up at me through a fringe of dark lashes. "I'm guessing you don't know your brother-in-law works for the Russian mob."

Chapter 16

THIS TIME I couldn't stifle the laugh. That was possibly the most ridiculous thing I'd ever heard. "Are you insane? My brother-in-law does not work for the Russian mob!"

Alex didn't even crack a smile. "How do you know?"

"Well, for one thing he doesn't speak Russian."

"They all speak English."

It didn't occur to me at the time to ask how he knew that. "And for another he's ex-law enforcement."

Now it was Alex who laughed. "Right. Rich white lady can't imagine a cop might break the law. Especially not a white cop."

"First of all, I'm not rich. Second, this has nothing to do with race. Third, I know some cops break the law, but my brother-in-law's not one of them."

"How do you know?"

"Because I know my brother-in-law!" I wasn't under the illusion Jake was squeaky clean. It would not surprise me to learn he'd bent a few rules when he worked for the FBI. But a mobster? No way.

Alex leaned back in his chair. "It could've been your husband. They look alike."

The notion that Jonah was a mobster was even more preposterous than Jake. "Not possible. My husband was an accountant."

"Mobsters need accountants too. Someone's got to clean the money."

"He wasn't that kind of accountant. He set up tax shelters for rich people who didn't want to pay taxes."

"And you think mobsters want to pay taxes? Haven't you ever heard of Al Capone?"

I knew Al Capone went to prison for tax evasion as opposed to all his other crimes, but the notion of Jonah working for a modern-day Al Capone was laughable. Jonah was a straight arrow. That was one of his traits I loved most. Jonah would never have worked for mobsters. Never.

"My husband's clients were rich people, not criminals."

"How are you so sure they weren't criminals? Because they looked like your husband instead of like me?"

"No, because if they were criminals Jonah would've told me." He often regaled me with stories of client meetings he attended with Brian Sullivan. Brian did all the schmoozing but left it to Jonah to explain the structure of the tax shelters they provided. According to Jonah, most clients weren't interested in the details. As long as he assured them he could reduce their tax burden without triggering an IRS audit, they were happy. Very few cared to know how he achieved that end.

"Most of them came by their wealth the old fashioned way," I explained. "They inherited it. The rest were self-made."

"Mobsters are self-made."

The fact we were even having this conversation was ridiculous. "Did you ever actually see my brother-in-law with a mobster?"

"Yes."

"And was the guy in handcuffs at the time?"

"No. He was giving your brother-in-law orders."

"You're lying."

"Why would I lie?"

"I don't know. You tell me."

We stared at each other in silence until the realization hit me. Jake had worked as an undercover agent. That must've been what Alex witnessed. "How long ago was it you saw them together?"

Alex shrugged. "I don't know. I didn't write it down on my calendar."

"Guess. A year ago? Two years ago? Three years ago?"

"A couple years ago."

Then it couldn't have been Jake. He'd left the FBI shortly after Jonah and I had moved to Santa Veneta, which was more than three years ago. "And you remember someone you met once a couple of years ago? It must've been a memorable meeting."

"It wasn't. I'm good with faces. That's how I stay alive."

"And may I ask why *you* were meeting with a bunch of Russian mobsters?"

"No." Then he stood up and left the room without another word.

I jumped up and followed him to my front door. When he reached for the handle, I grabbed his arm. "You can't just leave."

He stared down at my hand as if surprised by its appearance there. Then he encircled my wrist with his fingers and forcibly removed my hand from his arm. He didn't hurt me, but we both knew he could've if he'd wanted to.

"What about the flash drive?" I asked.

"I can't help you," he said then walked out of my house, slamming the door shut in my face.

．　．　．

I was still enraged over my conversation with Alex when Brian Sullivan called. His tone wasn't as friendly today as it had been earlier in the week. He didn't even bother with the pleasantries.

"You gave the messenger the wrong flash drive," he said.

It took me a minute to even realize what he was talking about. "I did? Are you sure?"

"Yes. The thumb drive you gave us didn't match any of our recovery keys."

"Sorry. I told you I didn't know if it was Jonah's. I guess it wasn't."

"No, it was Jonah's. Or yours. It was filled with photos of you and your baby."

Shit. I knew he'd be able to check how much memory was used, but I didn't think he'd be able to actually see what was on it without the password. "Then I'd like it back. I probably—"

"Here's the curious part, Grace. All of those photos were saved to the drive the day you gave it to us."

My heart started pounding in my chest. I didn't realize that's something someone would be able to check. I thought it would only show the dates the photos were taken like it did on my phone. "Really? How weird."

"That's how I know you gave us the wrong drive. By accident, I'm sure."

"Of course, by accident," I said even though we both knew that was a lie. "The thing is, Brian, I don't have any other flash drives."

"Maybe you should check again," he said, a hint of menace in his voice. "Just to be sure. It could've fallen behind a desk or under a piece of furniture. These things turn up in the strangest places sometimes. Will you do me that favor?"

"Sure."

"Thank you, Grace. I appreciate it very much."

"Not a problem. But I can't do it tonight. I have plans."

"Tomorrow's fine," he said. "I can come over and help you search, if you'd like."

I did not want Brian Sullivan anywhere near my house. "No, that won't be necessary."

"Alright," Brian said. "Call me when you find it, and I'll come pick it up."

"Okay, but I wouldn't get your hopes up. If Jonah left another flash drive lying around the house, I think I would've found it by now."

"Maybe," he said. "Maybe not. Text me either way."

"Will do." I hesitated, then decided this was a question an innocent person would ask. "By the way, how did you open the flash drive without the recovery key?"

"It took us a while, but eventually we figured out the password."

"Really? How?" I didn't think anyone would be able to guess the password I'd given MJ to use.

Brian chuckled. "Using family member's birthdates in passwords is pretty common, Grace. That's actually why it took us as long as it did. Jonah knew better."

Jonah did, but I didn't. I thought I'd been clever using our birthdates in reverse. I didn't ask Brian how he knew my and Amelia's birthdates, and he didn't offer an explanation.

Chapter 17

I REALLY WANTED to cancel my date with Daniel. My thoughts were consumed with Alex's accusation that Jake was working for the Russian mob. I knew it couldn't be true. But I also couldn't come up with a reason why Alex would lie. He gained no advantage that I could see. There had to be a reasonable explanation, but I sure as hell couldn't figure it out.

I wasn't worried about Brian Sullivan. I'd text him tomorrow, tell him I'd searched the house again, and I'd found nothing. Even if he was sure I was lying, what was he going to do?

My immediate problem was Daniel. I knew if I tried to cancel, we'd have a fight, and I didn't have the energy for it. It was easier to take the path of least resistance. We were seeing a movie anyway, so not much conversation would be required. And maybe post-movie sex would relax me.

I should've known better than to think it would be that easy.

"DON'T TAKE this the wrong way, Grace. I'm very much enjoying our physical relationship."

"Mmmm," I murmured. Daniel's bed was so comfortable. If he'd just stop talking, I could easily fall asleep.

"But I want more."

I sighed. I'd just had an amazing orgasm and now he was ruining my post-coital bliss. I rolled over to face him. "I don't mean to be sexist, but isn't it the woman who's supposed to want more?"

"That is sexist."

I laughed. "You're right. I'm sorry." Then I laid my head on his chest and closed my eyes.

He pushed my head off of him and sat up. "Are you?"

I pulled the sheet around my bare breasts and sat up too. "Yes. I like you. Isn't it obvious?"

"I know you like sleeping with me. I'm not sure you like anything else about me."

I sighed. "Now you're just being ridiculous."

"Am I? What else do you like doing with me?"

"Did we not just see a movie together? And how many times have we had dinner this week?"

"Yes, you come to my house for dinner and sex. But it's only ever my house, never yours, and getting information out of you is like pulling teeth."

"That's not true."

"It is. I feel like I'm dating a CIA agent."

"Didn't I tell you MJ's uncle came to my house this afternoon?" Although I hadn't told him Alex had accused Jake of working for the Russian mob.

"Why can we never spend the night at your house? Why does it always have to be mine?"

"I told you why on our first date."

"Yes. First time since your husband died. That I understood. But it's been weeks, Grace, and I'm still not allowed over. But MJ's drug dealer uncle? Him you invite."

"First of all, I did not invite Alex. He invited himself. And second, I am not sleeping with MJ's uncle. We had a short conversation and he left."

"A short conversation that just had to take place inside your home. And do you really think it's wise to invite a drug dealer to your house?"

"I didn't invite him! And what is this obsession you have with my house?"

"It's not about your house. It's about you being so secretive about everything."

"What am I being secretive about? What is it that you want to know?"

He raised his hand and ticked off the reasons on his fingers. "You won't tell me why your aunt had to foster MJ and Sofia instead of you. You won't tell me why you gave them up when you clearly didn't want to. And I still don't understand this relationship you have with Tim and Richard."

"We're friends."

"I have several students in foster care, Grace. But I don't know any other former foster parent who has dinner once a week with the new foster parent. It's weird."

"It's not weird."

"Yeah, Grace, it is. And you know what else is weird? Your irrational hatred of the Wellstone Center. What is that about?"

I could feel the tears welling up in my eyes, but I kept them at bay. "I think I should leave." I grabbed my panties off the floor and pulled them on and headed to the hallway where the rest of my clothes were scattered across the hardwood floor where Daniel had discarded them after he'd peeled them off me.

Daniel appeared behind me in the hallway wearing only his briefs. "Don't leave."

"I don't want to fight with you," I said, clasping my bra closed.

"I don't want to fight with you either. Grace, sweetheart, I think I'm falling in love with you."

That stopped me in my tracks. I managed to finish pulling my shirt over my head, but I wasn't sure what to do next. My jeans were still crumpled on the floor next to me, but reaching for them now, after his declaration, seemed like the wrong move. "I don't know what to say."

"It's okay. You don't have to say it back."

No, but he clearly wanted me to. No one says *I love you* or even *I think I'm falling in love with you* without wanting it reciprocated.

He kicked my jeans further down the hall and stood in front of me. When he placed his hands on my shoulders, I could feel the heat from his palms through my thin cotton shirt. "I'm not trying to rush you. I know you still have some things to work out."

That was one way to describe never-ending grief.

"I just need to know I have a chance."

"There's no one else, Daniel. There hasn't been since Jonah died." But as the words left my mouth, I thought of Jake and the night of my suicide attempt. But Jake was no threat to Daniel. We hadn't spoken in months.

My memory of that night must've shown on my face because Daniel wrapped his arms around me and said, "I'm sorry. I didn't mean to make you think of him."

You didn't; I was thinking of his brother. Then I instantly felt guilty, not for what I'd almost done that night with Jake, but for what I was currently doing to Daniel. He was right. I was keeping secrets from him. A lot of secrets. And I didn't know why. If I trusted him enough to sleep with him, shouldn't I trust him enough to confide in him?

Yes, you should. So why don't you?

I sighed and sat down on the floor. Daniel sat down next to

me and held my hand. Eventually, I worked up the nerve to tell him about my suicide attempt. After I answered all his questions, he led me back into the bedroom. This time it felt like more than just sex. Not love, but something more than just a physical release, which is what sex with Daniel had been for me. Afterwards, instead of retreating to separate sides of the bed, we fell asleep wrapped in each other's arms.

But when I woke up in the morning, we were on opposite sides of the bed again, and I was ravenous. I stretched my arms and legs and waited for Daniel to stir. Then I got tired of waiting and nudged him awake.

"Breakfast?" I asked when his eyes fluttered open.

"Sure." He yawned. "The pancake place or the beach café?"

"Actually, I was thinking we could have breakfast at my house." It wasn't a conscious decision. But sometime during the night I'd decided I needed to give this fledgling relationship a chance. It had been almost two years since Jonah died. It was time.

Daniel's eyes opened a little wider. "Your house?"

"Yes. I do know how to cook, even if it's not something I make a habit of. Although I was thinking we could just pick up bagels on the way."

A huge grin spread across his face. "Does this mean I finally get to see your bedroom?"

"Maybe. If you play your cards right."

Daniel was the first to spot the broken glass.

Chapter 18

"What happened here?" Daniel asked as we strolled into my kitchen with his arm around my shoulder and mine around his waist.

I placed the bag of bagels on the counter and followed Daniel's gaze to the laundry room. One of the glass panels in the back door had been smashed and the shards were lying on the floor.

"What the hell?" I walked into the laundry room and bent down. Then Daniel yelled, "Don't touch it," and I jumped back.

I hadn't been planning on touching the glass, but "Why not?"

"You need to call the police."

We searched the entire house while we waited for the police to arrive. Nothing appeared to be missing, or even out of place. Even my jewelry box was in the exact same spot on my dresser it always sat, my diamond engagement ring and wedding band still tucked into their nook. When I closed the jewelry box and turned around, I found Daniel lying in the middle of my bed with his hands folded behind his head. He'd kicked off his sneakers and they were strewn across the floor.

"I don't get it," I said, reaching down for his shoes and placing them next to the bed. "Why would someone break into my house and then not steal anything?"

"Beats me," Daniel replied.

I noticed he'd chosen the middle of the mattress rather than either side. Maybe he was afraid he'd accidentally choose Jonah's side and I'd get upset. I knew Daniel wanted me to sleep with him in that bed. For him it would prove I'd moved on from Jonah and was now emotionally available. I wanted to sleep with him in my bed too but for different reasons. I needed to exorcise my demons from the almost-night with Jake and my suicide attempt. We both would've gotten what we'd wanted today but for the break-in. Daniel appeared to still be willing, but I was no longer in the mood.

When the police finally arrived and I informed them nothing was missing, they immediately lost interest. They told me it was just neighborhood kids pulling a prank.

"Wouldn't neighborhood kids have messed up the house?" I asked. "Or at least turned on the TV and put their feet up on the furniture?" Other than the broken glass in the laundry room, there was no evidence anyone had been in my home.

"Best not to try to divine the motives of teenagers," the male cop said. "Just be thankful they didn't pee on your floor and kill your pets."

My jaw dropped. When I was a kid, pulling a prank involved toilet paper or ordering a dozen pizzas to someone's house. When did peeing on people's floors and killing their pets become a thing? "Teenagers do that now?" If MJ ever did that, I'd ground him for life, even if I wasn't his foster parent.

The female cop said, "The incident my partner was referring to wasn't teenagers. It was a mentally unstable individual who we suspect was on drugs at the time."

That didn't make me feel any safer. "Please tell me you caught the guy and he's in jail."

The partners exchanged a look and the male cop said, "You should install a home security system. Maybe buy a dog."

"Buy a dog?"

"They can be very effective deterrents," the female cop said.

The male cop nodded. "Big dogs are best. Not those teacup breeds."

I thanked them for their time and walked them to the front door. When they were gone, Daniel helped me clean up the broken glass and tape cardboard over the hole.

"Want to go back to my place?" Daniel asked.

"Would you mind?" Even if the person who'd broken into my house hadn't stolen anything, I still felt unsafe. Maybe it was time for me to sell the house and move. Although I had no idea where I'd move to. Where was safe anymore?

Daniel picked up the unopened bag of bagels from the kitchen counter. "I don't know if we can find a glass repair shop that's open on Sunday, but we can definitely buy you a home security system."

"No dog?" I asked.

"Sorry, I'm allergic."

Clearly, he thought he'd be sticking around for a while.

I texted MJ the next afternoon and told him to meet me at my house after school instead of the office because I was still waiting for the glass repair person to arrive.

"What's up with the camera?" he asked, pointing to the doorbell device Daniel had installed for me the night before, along with motion-activated lights and broken-glass sensors.

I held open the front door and motioned for him to come inside. "Someone broke in over the weekend. Nothing was stolen. The cops think it was neighborhood kids pulling a prank. You would never do anything like that, right?"

"Heck no. If I was gonna break into someone's house, I would steal something for sure."

"MJ!"

He laughed. "I'm just messing with you."

"Yeah, I know," I said as I locked the door behind him. "But it's not funny."

He gave me a sheepish grin. "Sorry."

MJ followed me into the kitchen and headed straight to the refrigerator. "You got anything to eat?"

"Just healthy stuff." If I knew we were meeting at my place today, I would've bought a bag of chips. I normally don't keep junk food in the house.

"S'okay," he said, pulling a large red apple out of the fruit bin. It sounded so crisp and crunchy when he took a bite I had him grab me one too.

"How's baby Aaron?" I asked as we sat at the kitchen table munching on our apples.

MJ swallowed hard. "He cries a lot."

"All babies cry a lot."

"Sofia didn't."

He could be forgetting, most of us do, or maybe it was a sign of something, although I didn't know what. I'd have to ask Tim if Sofia was having any problems in school. "Does he have colic?"

"I dunno," MJ said then took another bite of his apple.

"How are Tim and Richard doing?" I hadn't seen them much the last few weeks because they'd been consumed with the baby and I'd been consumed with Daniel.

MJ shrugged. "Fighting some."

They were probably both exhausted. I still remembered how tired I'd been with Amelia. When I drove MJ home, I'd stop in and offer to babysit. Even just a few hours of downtime can help.

MJ and I worked on his *Great Gatsby* essay while we waited for the glass repair person. When my back door no longer had a hole in it, I drove MJ back to Tim and Richard's house. It was even more chaotic than usual, and Tim looked frazzled. As MJ had predicted, baby Aaron was crying.

"May I?" I held my hands out for Aaron, who Tim was holding in one arm, while stirring something on the stove with the other.

"Sure." He seemed relieved to pass him off to me.

"What's wrong, Aaron?" I asked as I stared into his beautiful brown eyes.

He cried in response.

I checked his diaper, which was dry, then tried lifting him up and down like Jonah used to do with Amelia. That quieted him, but as soon as I stopped, he started crying again. "Have you tried the vacuum cleaner?" I asked Tim.

He looked up from the stove. "Is that a joke?"

"No. Didn't you read the book about the fourth trimester?"

"Look at this place," Tim snapped. "Do I look like I have time to read books?"

It was the first time he'd ever raised his voice to me, and I was taken aback.

"Sorry," he said. "I'm just so tired. I feel like I'm losing my mind."

I stared into his exhausted face and the memories of those first few months with Amelia came rushing back to me. There were times I would literally beg her to stop crying and I would've done anything to get her to go to sleep.

I turned off the stove and took the spoon from Tim's hand. "Go take a nap. I'll watch Aaron."

"I don't have time for a nap. I still need to cook dinner, fold the laundry, help Isaiah with his homework, finish an art project with Makeyla, and about a million other things."

"Who wants pizza for dinner?" I called out.

A chorus of *Me* rose from the living room.

I turned back to Tim. "Well, you can cross dinner off your list. Now go upstairs and take a nap." When he started to protest, I cut him off. "I'm not taking no for an answer."

I thought he might yell at me again, but he looked like he was about to cry. "Thank you," he said, then kissed both me and Aaron on the top of the head before heading up the steps.

RICHARD ARRIVED home two hours later to a stack of empty pizza boxes and a still awake but not crying baby. I'd put MJ in charge of keeping Aaron entertained while I folded the laundry. MJ was now the oldest child in the house since Jayden had turned eighteen last week and had moved out.

"Where's Tim and the baby?" Richard asked.

Naturally, he assumed the two were together, which was part of the problem. "MJ's watching Aaron and Tim's upstairs sleeping."

Richard lifted the lid on one of the pizza boxes.

"I saved you two slices. They're in the fridge. And I put a beer in the freezer."

"Bless you," he said and headed to the refrigerator.

I waited until he sat down at the kitchen counter and took a sip of his beer before I said, "We need to talk."

His shoulders sagged. "Can I at least eat first? I'm starving."

I smiled remembering Jonah saying the same to me once in what felt like another lifetime. I nodded to the two slices of pizza. "Do you want me to heat those up for you?"

"Nah, I like it cold," he said and bit into a slice of pepperoni.

Jonah would eat cold pizza too. I preferred mine hot.

I waited until Richard finished eating before I laid into him. "You need to help Tim more. He can't take care of Aaron, the house, and the rest of the kids all on his own."

I thought he might tell me to mind my own business, that it wasn't my place to interfere, which was true. But if not me, then who? Richard's closest relative was a cousin who lived in Fresno. Both of Tim's parents were still alive, but they lived in Ohio and, apparently, did not feel the need to come out to California to meet their new grandson. I wasn't surprised since Tim had told me he had a strained relationship with them. What Tim and Richard needed was an interfering mother, like mine. Since neither of them had one, I stepped in to fill the gap.

Richard didn't get angry with me, but he said, "Tim and I agreed that he should be the one to get up with the baby during the night because I have to go to work in the morning."

I recalled having this same argument with Jonah. "Taking care of a baby is work too, except you don't get to leave at the end of the day. You just work around the clock." The solution for me and Jonah had been to hire a baby nurse for two weeks. After that my mother came down from San Francisco for a month to help out. But I knew neither of those scenarios were an option for Tim and Richard.

"I can't afford to take time off," Richard said, a peevish tone creeping in. "So what do you suggest?"

A baby swing, a white noise machine, and setting up a schedule for the rest of the kids to watch Aaron in the afternoons so Tim could get a break. I also offered to babysit the following weekend. Unlike with the baby furniture, I didn't have to push Richard to accept my offer. He said yes immediately.

· · ·

WHEN I FINALLY LEFT TIM AND Richard's house later that night, I was too tired to see Daniel. I knew he'd be angry when I cancelled, so I sent him a text message then shut off my phone. After I'd taken a long hot shower, changed into pajamas, and slid into bed, I called him to apologize. He softened when I promised he could come over the following night.

"I still think it's weird you're such good friends with them," Daniel said.

I yawned into the phone. "You're just mad because I went to their house tonight instead of yours." I knew it wasn't about me or them. Daniel was upset because we still hadn't christened my bed.

"No," Daniel said, "I really don't get it. Why are you doing this?"

"What am I doing? A couple of hours of babysitting? A few loads of laundry?" That was nothing compared to taking care of a newborn, especially when you had four other kids in the house.

"No, this relationship. You literally have nothing in common with them other than MJ and his sister, and they're not even yours anymore."

He'd brought up my supposedly weird friendship with Tim and Richard enough times now that I'd actually given it some thought. I'd even discussed it with Dr. Rubenstein, who'd agreed with me.

"I told you. Tim and Richard take in strays." My word, not theirs. If you asked them, they would say they help people and pets in need. "When I showed up on their doorstep with Sofia's dollhouse, Tim took me in. He and Richard recognized my need to be part of a family again, so they invited me into theirs. It really is that simple."

"Don't you want a family of your own?"

"I have family. But my mom lives in San Francisco and my

aunt is busy with her own life." Which reminded me that I needed to call her back. I'd been putting it off because I knew she wanted to meet Daniel, and I wasn't sure I was ready to introduce them.

"I meant kids," Daniel said.

Of course, I immediately thought of Amelia. I couldn't imagine having another child. Yet, I couldn't imagine *not* having another child. "Someday, yes, but for right now I'm happy being a part of their family."

Before Daniel could reply my phone beeped with a call from MJ. He should've been asleep already so naturally my mind jumped to worst case scenarios. "I have to go," I said and hung up on Daniel so I could answer MJ's call.

Chapter 19

"What's wrong?" I asked. "Is the baby okay?"

"Yeah," MJ replied. "He cried for a while, but he finally fell asleep."

My heart slowly returned to its normal beats per minute. "It's pretty late. Shouldn't you be asleep too?" I didn't know whether Tim and Richard had imposed a bedtime on MJ, but I knew how early in the morning he had to get up for school.

"Uncle Alex told me to call you. He said to give you a message." I heard paper rustling and MJ sounded like he was reading. "Get it out of your house."

"Get what out of my house?"

"I don't know. He wouldn't tell me. He just said to give you this message and you'd understand."

"Well, I don't understand. And why didn't he just call me himself? Why'd he have you call?"

"I dunno," MJ said.

This whole thing was weird. But I was too tired to figure it out. "Was that it? Everything else okay?"

"Yup, that was it. See you at the office tomorrow?"

"Yes." I was about to say goodnight when a thought

occurred to me. "You didn't tell your uncle about the break-in, did you?"

"Yeah," MJ said. "Was I not supposed to? I didn't know it was a secret."

"It's not a secret. I'm just wondering why you told him."

"He asked how you were doing, and I told him some dumb ass broke into your house and didn't steal nothing. You think the message has something to do with that?"

"I have no idea," I said, but I was wondering the same thing. The neighborhood kids pulling a prank theory never made sense to me. But I could imagine someone breaking in looking for something specific, then leaving when he didn't find it because that something was still in the zippered compartment of my purse. "When you talk to your uncle, does he usually ask about me?"

"I dunno. Why? You want me to tell him you was asking about him? I don't think Mr. Guardia's gonna like that."

I laughed. "What do you know about me and Mr. Guardia?" MJ had been there the day we ran into each other at the beach, but he hadn't seen us together since.

"I hear things," he said. "I got ears, ya know."

I didn't need to see the grin on his face. I could hear it in his voice. "Oh yeah, what kind of things?"

MJ made smooching sounds into the phone, and I laughed again.

"You're pretty good at that. You wouldn't be practicing on Olivia, would you?"

I imagined MJ turning bright red because that's what happened the last time I asked him about Olivia. Although he swore they weren't dating, just hanging out together sometimes. Whatever that meant. I received a similar answer when I'd asked Olivia about MJ.

"Goodnight, Lawyer Mom," MJ said in a singsong voice.

"Goodnight, MJ."

I was smiling when I ended the call, but then I thought of Alex's cryptic message and my smile disappeared. The "it" Alex wanted out of my house had to be the flash drive. There was nothing else. But why did he think whatever was on the flash drive was valuable enough to steal? He had no more knowledge of what it contained than I did.

I considered calling Daniel back but dismissed the idea. I knew if I told him about MJ's message, he would get mad at me all over again that I'd allowed Alex to come to my house, then he'd tell me the break-in had nothing to do with the flash drive and I was being paranoid.

I hoped he was right about the paranoia because the alternative was terrifying. If someone was willing to break into my house to steal the flash drive, what else were they willing to do?

Chapter 20

I STOPPED at the bank the next morning. Maybe Alex was being paranoid and maybe I was too, but it wouldn't hurt to err on the side of caution. My safe deposit box was the most secure place I could think of to store the flash drive until I could figure out what to do next.

After the bank manager directed me to a tiny windowless room, I lifted the lid on the long metal safe deposit box and pulled out the contents one by one. The last time I'd opened the box was the week after Jonah and Amelia's funeral. That's when I'd discovered the second life insurance policy. I didn't expect to find anything that earth shattering today. No open-in-the-event-of-my-death letter I'd somehow missed before. But I did wonder if perhaps Jonah had left something inside the box that in my haze of shock and grief I'd overlooked. Something that could help explain why he felt the need to tape a flash drive to the bottom of Amelia's diaper caddy.

I pulled out all three of our birth certificates, social security cards, copies of our passports, my grandmother's pearls, and the deed to our house. There were no post-it notes stuck between the pages or passwords written in the margins. Nothing was amiss. I stared at the copy of Jonah's passport. The photo was old, taken before we got engaged, when our future together was filled with possibility. I would never have imagined ten years later Jonah wouldn't be alive to renew.

I smiled as I remembered how Jonah had fooled me with this passport. It was my birthday and we'd gone to one of those special-occasion restaurants for dinner. When he placed the flat rectangular box on the table while we waited for our dessert, I'd thought he'd bought me the pendant necklace he knew I wanted. We'd spotted it together when we'd been out shopping a few weeks earlier. I'd tried it on and asked him if he thought I should buy it. He was noncommittal, which I'd interpreted as *maybe I'll buy it for you* since my birthday was coming up.

The box was the right size and shape for a necklace, so when I'd ripped off the silver wrapping paper and lifted the lid, I was sure I was going to find the pendant inside. I didn't even try to hide my disappointment as I unfolded the tissue paper and discovered the slim blue book. "Oh. You finally got a passport."

I'd been surprised when he first told he didn't have a passport. My parents got me one when I was a baby. Jonah had explained he'd only left the country once on a road trip to Mexico with his brother, and at the time you didn't need a passport if you crossed the southern border by land.

I'd checked underneath the passport, hoping there were some airline tickets too, but there weren't any. The box was empty.

"I thought you'd be happy," he said, taking in the, no doubt, unhappy expression on my face. "Now we can travel."

"I am happy," I lied.

"Damnit, I knew I should've bought you that necklace."

I shrugged. I'd just buy it for myself. I should've done so to begin with instead of hoping he'd take the hint.

Then the waiter arrived with a plate of profiteroles, which he set down in the center of the table with two forks. I tasted them first and moaned. "These are so good."

Jonah took a bite. "Not bad."

"Not bad? Are you kidding me?" Jonah wasn't a dessert person. He only ordered it for me.

"You think they're as good here as they are in France?"

"How would I know," I mumbled with my mouth full of pastry. I'd only been to France once, when I was seven. My parents were forced to take me on their long-planned anniversary trip because my aunt, who was supposed to babysit me while they were away, got stuck in some war-torn country and couldn't get back in time. All I really remembered about France were the many art museums my parents dragged me to and then not getting to see the Palace of Versailles, the one tourist site I'd actually wanted to visit, because we'd gotten lost on our last day in Paris and missed the train.

"I think we should find out. *Tu veux aller à Paris avec moi?*"

Would you like to go to Paris with me? I knew that's what Jonah had been trying to say. But Jonah had never learned French in school and didn't know the accent, so it sounded more like *Two-vex-allery-Paris-ovek-mwa.*

I swallowed my profiterole and said, "I would love to go to Paris with you."

Jonah's shoulders dropped several inches and he sighed. "Thank god. Because the tickets I bought are non-refundable."

I smiled to myself as I let the memory of our trip wash over me. Jonah made sure this time I got to see the Palace of Versailles. He had the hotel concierge mark the route to the train station on our map, then write down exactly which train we were supposed to take and the time schedule. We visited the Palace of Versailles on our first full day in Paris, even before we visited the Eiffel Tower.

Jonah proposed to me on the patio overlooking the palace's gardens. When he dropped down on one knee with a blue velvet box and I said yes, all the other visitors clapped, even the ones who didn't speak English.

"Tu me manques, mon amour," I whispered to the photocopy of Jonah's passport, then I kissed the grainy black and white image of his face. After I wiped my eyes, I placed all the documents back in the box. Then I reached into the zippered compartment of my purse for the flash drive and placed it on top. I closed the lid on the metal box and stood up to leave when I had an idea.

Chapter 21

I SAT DOWN and pulled my laptop out of my briefcase. I plugged the flash drive into the USB port and typed *Tu veux aller à Paris avec moi?* into the password bar and pressed enter. Of course, it didn't work. I retyped it without any spaces or accent marks. The same error message I'd received thousands of times before popped up on the screen. I tried again in English. Also incorrect. I was about to give up when it occurred to me Jonah would've used an online translator. I knew from experience those translations were often different than the way they teach you to speak the language in school.

There was no wi-fi signal in the windowless room, but I still had cell service on my phone. I typed *Would you like to go to Paris with me?* into an English-to-French translator and, as I suspected, the translation it spit out was slightly different than what I'd tried. I typed the new translation, minus the spaces and accent marks, into the password box and tapped the enter key.

To my complete and utter amazement, the drive unlocked.

Chapter 22

THE FLASH DRIVE contained only one file—a spreadsheet. I clicked on the file and stared at the columns of numbers and letters with no names and no discernible pattern.

Account numbers? Maybe. But if so, wouldn't there be names attached to them? And what bank issued alpha-numeric account numbers fifty characters long? Plus, the letters and numbers were so random they seemed more like really long computer-generated passwords. But passwords to what?

I had no idea what any of this information was and, more importantly, what I was supposed to do with it. But I was meeting with a new client on the other side of town in half an hour and I didn't have time to figure it out now. I saved the file to my laptop, dropped the flash drive into the safe deposit box, and left the bank.

My meeting ran long, and I barely arrived at the courthouse in time for my court appearance, then I had to rush back to the office to finish drafting a status report that needed to be filed with the court by the end of the day. By the time I returned Daniel's call, the sun was low on the horizon.

"Hey, babe," he answered. "I was just thinking about you."

"Oh? What were you thinking?" I was thinking I could really use one of his amazing scalp massages.

"That I didn't know what wine to bring because I didn't know what you were cooking."

Damnit. I'd forgotten I'd offered to cook dinner tonight. "About that—"

"Jesus, Grace, you're not cancelling on me again?"

Merely sleeping with me wasn't good enough anymore, Daniel had to sleep with me *in my bed.* This had become a quest for him, like completing a triathlon, which he was training for too. "Calm down. I'm not cancelling. I just had a really busy day and don't feel like cooking. I was calling to ask what kind of takeout you wanted."

"Oh. Sorry," he said sheepishly. "I didn't mean to yell at you."

"It's okay."

No, it's not, I chastised myself. *You've been dating the man for a month, and he's already yelled at you multiple times.*

You and Jonah fought sometimes too. Your marriage wasn't perfect.

Jonah wasn't controlling.

Daniel's not controlling.

Oh no? Then why does he keep haranguing you about your supposedly weird relationship with Tim and Richard?

He's just jealous.

Why would he be jealous of your friendship with two gay men? There's something wrong with him. This isn't normal.

"Hello, hello. Are you there?" Daniel asked, forcing me to focus on his words instead of my own thoughts.

"Sorry, my phone cut out. What did you say?"

"I said I'd pick up dinner on the way to your house. Just tell me what time to be there."

. . .

DANIEL ARRIVED at eight o'clock with kabob platters from the Greek restaurant and a bottle of Chardonnay. He kissed me hello then said, "You're all I've thought about today. I can't wait to get you upstairs."

I knew I should be flattered, but all I felt was stressed.

Maybe you're not ready for a relationship.

Maybe you should drink some wine and think about how great that scalp massage is going to feel.

I took my own advice. I drank a glass of the buttery Chardonnay and tried to focus my thoughts on the extremely enjoyable aspects of our relationship. But my mind kept wandering to Jonah's spreadsheet and what all those letters and numbers could possibly mean. I managed to pay attention to Daniel when he told me a story about one of his students who was struggling with algebra. Then I told him about my new client, a fifteen-year-old boy whose parents were using him as a pawn in their divorce.

We finished eating and I loaded our dirty plates and silverware into the dishwasher. Then we took our glasses and the remaining half bottle of wine into the living room. That's when I told Daniel I'd finally guessed the password to Jonah's flash drive.

"You're kidding. What was it?"

"A question that meant something to us but no one else would ever guess. And he wrote it in French and spelled it wrong."

Daniel laughed. "Next to using a computer-generated password, a passphrase is the most secure. Props to your husband for writing it in a foreign language and spelling it wrong too." Daniel laughed again and so did I.

"Well done, Jonah." I lifted my wineglass and Daniel clinked his against mine and we both took a sip.

"How did you finally figure it out?" Daniel asked.

"It was completely random," I said, setting my wineglass on the coffee table. "I went to the bank this morning to put the flash drive in our safe deposit box and—"

"Wait, you have a safe deposit box?"

"Yeah, doesn't everyone?" My mom and my aunt both do.

Daniel shook his head. "No. Sorry. Please continue."

"Well, after the break-in Alex thought I shouldn't keep the flash drive in the house anymore so I—"

"Hang on," Daniel said and set his wineglass down too. "You're referring to MJ's uncle, right?"

"Right. I called him to see if he knew a hacker, remember?"

"I remember. And he invited himself over to your house because for some reason he couldn't discuss it with you over the phone."

Of course, Daniel remembered that part. "Yes. Then MJ told him about the break-in and—"

"Time out," Daniel said, making a T-shape with his hands as if he was a referee. "Why would MJ tell his uncle about the break-in?"

"I don't know. He just did."

"And why did you tell MJ?"

"I didn't plan to but when he came here yesterday and saw the doorbell camera, he asked about it so—"

"MJ comes here too? I thought he works for you at your office."

"He does. Normally. But I was stuck here all afternoon waiting for the glass guy, so I told him to come here instead. Now do you want to hear the story or not?"

"I do. Please continue." Then Daniel picked up his glass and swirled the wine a few times before taking another sip.

"So, MJ told his uncle about the break-in and Alex didn't think it was kids pulling a prank either."

Daniel's eyebrows shot up. "Either?"

"Well, yeah. I mean, why would neighborhood kids break into my house as a prank? I don't even know any of the kids in this neighborhood."

Daniel set his wineglass down again. "Let me make sure I understand. You and Alex think bored teenagers looking for trouble is far-fetched, but someone breaking into your house to steal a flash drive you didn't even know existed until a week ago makes sense?"

Well, when you put it that way... "It's possible."

Daniel scoffed. "Grace, why would someone want to steal your flash drive?"

"Because of what's on it. Obviously."

"You don't even know what's on it."

"Well, I do now." I stomped out of the room, retrieved my laptop from my briefcase, and returned with it to the living room where Daniel was now scrolling on his phone. I turned on the computer, clicked on the file I'd copied from Jonah's flash drive, and turned the screen so it was facing Daniel. "See for yourself."

Daniel slipped his phone into his pocket and pulled the computer onto his lap. "What am I looking at?"

"I don't know. That's the problem."

"You don't know what this is, but you think it's worth stealing?"

Daniel was starting to remind me of Dr. Stetler. I wanted to smack his smug face. "Obviously, *someone* knows what it is."

"Yeah," Daniel said, "and that *someone* is dead."

"And maybe that someone is dead because of what's in this file."

Daniel looked up from the screen and stared at me. "Are you serious?"

It was the first time I'd said it out loud, but the thought had been percolating in my head all day. "I don't know. Maybe."

"Then you must have some guess as to what you think this is."

I hesitated, wondering how much I should share with Daniel. But I'd gone this far. I might as well go all the way. "At first I thought it was a list of account numbers. But every bank account number I've ever had is just a list of numbers, not letters too, and never this long. Now I'm thinking maybe they're passwords."

"Passwords to what?"

"I have no idea."

Daniel scrolled down to the bottom of the spreadsheet and back up to the top again. "You know what these look like to me?"

"No, what?"

"Private keys."

Chapter 23

"What's a private key?" I asked.

Daniel drained his wineglass and moved it off to the side, then placed the open laptop in the center of coffee table. "You know what cryptocurrency is, right?"

"You mean Bitcoin?" I didn't own any and didn't really understand how it worked, but I knew lots of people thought it was valuable and some of those people had made a ton of money investing in it.

"Bitcoin is one form of cryptocurrency, but there are lots of others. Do you know how digital currencies work?"

"No clue."

Daniel started by explaining blockchains and smart contracts, and by the time he got to the cryptographic algorithm hash, I was hopelessly confused. "Can you please just tell me what a private key is?"

"Essentially, it's a password. When you purchase cryptocurrency, you get two keys—a public key and a private key. Both are alphanumeric strings like these," he said, gesturing to the spreadsheet. "Think of the public key like an email address or a phone number. You can give it out to anyone. But the private key works like a password, so you need to safeguard it. To access a digital wallet, you need both the public key and the private key."

"So it's like a safe deposit box at the bank? You need both keys to open it?"

"No, because the public key is information anyone can get. Only the bank has access to the bank's safe deposit key. But you do need both keys to open a digital wallet, so in that sense, they're the same."

"You're saying if someone knows my public key and then they find my private key, they can open my digital wallet and steal all my money?"

"Yes. But unlike money held in a bank, there's no central clearinghouse for cryptocurrencies. If someone steals your digital currency, you have no recourse; there's no one to call to get your money back."

"What happens if I lose my key?" I'd forgotten my passwords plenty of times.

"This is one password you definitely don't want to lose. You can't access your digital wallet without the private key. And it's not just cryptocurrencies that work this way. It's NFTs too. You know what those are, right?"

"Um, sort of." I'd heard the phrase before, of course, but I didn't actually know what the letters stood for.

Daniel pulled my computer into his lap and started typing. Then he turned the screen to face me. I was staring at a gallery of digital artwork. "All of these are NFTs," he said. "Non-fungible tokens."

"Digital prints?" I asked.

"Not prints. They're digital only."

"So I can't buy one of these and have it shipped to me?"

"When you buy an NFT, all you're buying is a digital token on a blockchain."

"And what can I do with that?"

"Hold onto it, trade it, hope it goes up in value."

"Like a baseball card, but digital only, no physical card?"

"No, the artist who created these might have physical copies, but you're only buying a digital one."

"What's to stop the artist from making and selling more digital copies?"

"Nothing."

This was making my head hurt. "I don't understand. If the artist can make more NFTs whenever they want, then why does *my* NFT have value?"

"Why does any art have value? Because people think it does." Daniel reached for the laptop again and pulled up a video of two toddlers fighting, which I vaguely remembered watching when the clip had gone viral a couple of years ago.

"That one sold for over half a million dollars."

"No way! I watched it for free."

"You can still watch it for free."

"Then why would someone pay half a million dollars for it?"

"Because now they own it."

This felt like a giant Ponzi scheme. "I think I'm in the wrong business. I should be making viral videos and selling them as NFTs."

Daniel laughed. "A lot of people feel that way right now."

I reached for the laptop and clicked on the spreadsheet again. "You really think these are private keys?"

He shrugged. "Possibly. Or they could be public keys, in which case they're worthless."

"Aren't they worthless either way? I mean, even if they're private keys, I have no way of knowing which accounts, or digital wallets, they unlock."

"No, because unlike a typical password, a private key is tied to a public key."

I stared at him, even more confused now than I was before.

"A public key without the corresponding private key is worthless," he explained. "But if you have someone's private key, it's possible to reverse engineer their public key. Then you'd have both keys, and you could access their digital wallet."

I rubbed my temples and took a deep breath. This was all so confusing. "Okay, let's assume for the sake of argument this is a list of private keys. What do I do with them?"

"That depends. Do you want to steal other people's crypto and NFTs?"

"No!" We hadn't known each other long, but I would've hoped he knew at least that much about me.

"Then you have two choices. You can either give the file to your husband's former boss—"

"No."

Daniel's eyebrows shot up. "Why not?"

I ignored his question. "What's the other choice?"

"Delete the file."

"I can't."

"Why? If you're not planning on reverse engineering them so you can access the digital wallets they're tied to, then they are worthless."

I stared at him with my lips sealed. I hadn't told Daniel that Alex accused Jake of working with the Russian mob or that Brian Sullivan had figured out I'd given him the wrong flash drive. And I had no desire to share that information with him now. "I just can't."

"Grace, if these really are private keys, then the owners of these keys will want them back. They can't access their digital wallets without them."

I kept my lips pressed together.

"If you really believe someone broke into your house to try to steal this file, then don't you think keeping it is dangerous? Maybe you should turn it over to the police."

"I'm not giving it to the police. Not yet at least."

"Why?"

"What do you think the police are going to do with it? They told me the break-in was neighborhood kids pulling a prank."

"Then call the FBI."

And possibly implicate Jake? No way. I still didn't believe he was working for the Russian mob, but it wouldn't surprise me to learn he'd done something he shouldn't have. "No."

Daniel threw his arms up. "What reason could you possibly have for wanting to hold onto this file? It's worthless to you and potentially dangerous."

"Because it's the only lead I have."

"Lead to what?"

"To finding out why Jonah and Amelia were murdered."

Chapter 24

Daniel held up his hands as if they could physically stop my train of thought from running over him. "Hold on. You told me the guy who killed them was nuts. That they were just in the wrong place at the wrong time."

"Because that's what the police told me."

"And you think the police lied to you?" Daniel said, incredulous.

"I'm not saying anyone lied *intentionally*. Maybe they just got it wrong. Maybe we all did." I jumped up from the couch and started pacing the living room. I felt like I was trying to put together a jigsaw puzzle, but I was missing too many pieces and there was no picture on the box to guide me. Yet I could no longer ignore all these coincidences.

"Grace, do you think maybe you're overreacting?"

"I'm not overreacting!" I screeched.

"Sorry, wrong word. What I meant was you're jumping to a lot of conclusions—and I think I know why."

His condescending tone was really starting to grate on me. "Do you now?"

"Yes." He leaned back, spreading both arms along the top of

the couch, clearly pleased with himself. "You're still searching for meaning in your family's death. You can't accept that there is none."

I stopped pacing and stared at him. "What on earth are you talking about?"

He leaned forward, eager to explain. "After we started seeing each other, I did a little reading up on grieving."

Reading up on grieving? "Excuse me?"

"I wanted to learn more about it. So I could help you."

"Help me how?"

"Based on the data, people who lose a loved one suddenly, especially if it's a violent death like it was for your family, grieve longer. The researchers concluded it's because they have a harder time making sense of the loss. They're constantly searching for meaning where none exists."

Based on the data? I stared at him with my mouth ajar.

He stood up and walked toward me, but left some distance between us as if I was a wild animal he was trying to assist but didn't trust not to attack. "I want you to know I get it. I understand why you're doing this."

"Really?" I said, my voice dripping with sarcasm.

"Yes." He grabbed the laptop off the coffee table and held it in the space between us. "Grace, this is just a spreadsheet, nothing more. But you've convinced yourself it's the reason your family was killed. You've spun this elaborate tale that someone broke into your house to steal a flash drive."

"Someone did break into my house! You saw it yourself. You helped me clean up the broken glass."

Daniel set the laptop on the coffee table and took a step closer. "Grace, listen to yourself. It was neighborhood kids pulling a prank. Or maybe it was a burglar, but something scared him off. What I'm confident it wasn't was someone who broke into your house to steal a flash drive."

I backed away from him and found myself in the corner of the living room. "You think I'm some crazy tinfoil hat person, don't you?"

He paused then said, "You told me yourself you tried to commit suicide and you spent some time in an institution."

"So?"

"Grace, I think you need help."

He might as well have punched me in the stomach. The effect was the same. I grabbed my midsection and bent over. Then I looked up at his smug face. "It's time for you to leave."

Daniel took another step closer, boxing me in. "You don't mean that."

Intellectually, I knew I was free, but Daniel made me feel like I was back at the Wellstone Center being held against my will. Which turned out to be exactly the impetus I needed. I stood up straight, arms at my sides, fists clenched. "I think I know my own mind, Daniel. Now get the fuck out of my house before I call the police."

Chapter 25

"Wow," Dr. Rubenstein said.

I didn't have an appointment for today, but after I kicked Daniel out of my house last night, I really did feel like I was losing my mind. I'd paced for hours and when I finally went to bed, I just tossed and turned until the sun rose. After I eventually slept for a whole thirty minutes, I called Dr. Rubenstein and begged her to squeeze me in today. She'd agreed to see me during her lunch hour. Her untouched salad was still sitting on the desk behind her.

"Wow good or wow bad?" I asked.

She shifted in her chair. "Well, first, I'm proud of you for taking a stand with Daniel. I saw some red flags there and I'm glad you not only saw them but acted upon them. So many women just ignore the warning signs."

"It wasn't that hard. All I really liked about him was the sex."

"I am one hundred percent sure if all you want from a relationship is sex, you'll be able to find it easily enough. I'm more interested in why you lashed out at him."

I thought that part was obvious. "He basically called me crazy."

"You've said that about yourself many times."

"It's like the N-word. If you're crazy you can say it, but no one else can."

Dr. Rubenstein frowned. "No, Grace, it's not like the N-word."

She was right, of course. "Sorry, bad analogy, but you know what I mean." She wasn't letting me off the hook that easily though. We sat together in silence until I finally admitted in that moment, I felt like I was trapped in the Wellstone Center with Dr. Stetler. "But I wasn't going to give him that power over me. We were in my house and if I tell someone to leave, they have to go."

She nodded. "I commend you for standing up for yourself. But have you given any thought to what Daniel actually said? Just because he reminded you of Dr. Stetler, doesn't mean everything he told you was wrong."

"Now you think I'm crazy too? You think I need to check myself back into the Wellstone Center?"

"No and no. But I do think it's worth exploring what Daniel very unartfully tried to tell you."

"Which is?"

She stared directly at me. "Maybe the spreadsheet really is just a spreadsheet and not the linchpin in a criminal conspiracy that resulted in the death of your family."

It felt like my chest was being squeezed in a vise. It wasn't a complete shock Daniel wouldn't believe me. I'd withheld crucial information from him. Plus, he was a jerk. But Dr. Rubenstein knew everything, and up until now, I'd thought she was on my side. "You think I'm a whack job who just made this all up because I can't handle the fact that my family's dead?"

"Grace, I didn't—"

"You think I'm lying? That I fabricated a five-million-dollar life insurance policy? That I just imagined Jake appearing in my house that day?"

"No."

"I still don't know why he was there. He refused to tell me, and we haven't spoken since."

"Couldn't it be because he's embarrassed? Don't forget you rebuffed his advances and then tried to kill yourself. That's not a boost to anyone's ego. And didn't you tell me Jonah bought the life insurance policy right after Amelia was born? A lot of men feel a huge weight of responsibility when their first child is born. Buying the policy may just have been his way of dealing with it."

"What about the flash drive? Why password protect it and hide it somewhere no one would ever think to look if it's meaningless?"

"I add passwords to all my drives and devices. It's basic digital security."

"Because you're a doctor and your files contain confidential information."

"You're a lawyer. Don't your files contain confidential information? Jonah was an accountant. Didn't his files contain confidential information? To go from a file contains confidential information to someone is willing to kill for it is quite a leap."

"Then what about the break-in? Is that a leap too?"

"From what you told me, you were carrying the flash drive in your purse for days. Wouldn't the person who wanted to steal it know that?"

"No, why would they know that? I never said I thought someone was following me."

"Well, isn't it just as likely? If someone was following you, would you even know? And if someone really did break into your house to steal the flash drive and they didn't find it, wouldn't the next logical place to look for it be your office? Have you had a recent break-in at your office too?"

"No, but we have a lot of security at the office. My aunt made me set all that up before I rented the place."

Dr. Rubenstein sighed. "Grace, all I'm saying is there's no reason to think the file on that flash drive is somehow connected to Jonah and Amelia's death."

"Then why did Alex say all that stuff to me about the Russian mob and warn me I had to get the flash drive out of the house?"

"Honestly, I don't know. But why do you suddenly trust Alex? You never used to. What's changed, other than that he's telling you what you want to hear?"

"You think I want to hear that my brother-in-law works for the Russian mob?"

"I think you want to hear that Jonah and Amelia died for a reason; that it wasn't just bad luck. And that's completely normal, Grace. Human beings like to feel like we have control over our lives. We hate uncertainty. Think of all the ball players who believe in lucky socks or shorts or jerseys. Do you really think it's their clothes that make them win games?"

I could feel the tears prickling my eyes, but I kept them at bay. "No."

"Neither do I, but those ball players do. People would rather embrace a lie than accept life's uncertainty."

"But this isn't about lucky socks. It's a spreadsheet filled with passwords. A hidden flash drive—"

"Hidden or lost? Isn't it just as likely the flash drive fell out of Jonah's pocket when he was refilling the diaper caddy than he purposely hid it there? Maybe even more likely?"

"It was taped to the bottom! You think it fell in there with the tape attached?"

She shrugged, as if to say *maybe*.

"What about Jake sneaking into my house? I *know* he looked through Jonah's desk. The chair was still warm when I sat in it."

Dr. Rubenstein shook her head. "You don't know that, Grace. Yes, maybe the chair was warm because Jake sat in it. Or maybe it was warm because it was sitting in the sun. I can tell you if I leave those blinds open all day—" she nodded at the window behind me "—the couch you're sitting on gets warm too."

She was looking for reasons not to believe me. "Then why was Jake there?" I folded my arms across my chest and glared at her, daring her to come up with yet another excuse.

"Have you considered perhaps Jake came to your house that day because he was missing Jonah too? Maybe being at Jonah's house, sitting in Jonah's chair, looking through Jonah's desk, maybe all those things made him feel close to Jonah. And maybe, being who he is, Jake was too embarrassed to admit that to you."

"And fucking Jonah's wife? Did he want to do that to make him feel closer to Jonah too?"

Dr. Rubenstein sighed but didn't answer me. Instead, she said, "I'm sorry, but our time is up."

ME WALKING out of Dr. Rubenstein's office in tears was not unusual. What was unusual was feeling like she was gaslighting me. Yes, I knew there were alternative explanations for each piece of evidence I offered up. But offering up alternative theories is what defense attorneys did every day—and their clients still got convicted. It was the *quantity* of circumstantial evidence that swayed juries. And it was the quantity of these seeming coincidences that was swaying me.

At this point, there was only one person I wanted to talk to —the only one I knew who would believe me.

Chapter 26

I DROVE DIRECTLY from Dr. Rubenstein's office to the Winston Academy. The car pick-up line snaked outside the school gate and around the block. I parked across the street and texted MJ. *Want a ride?*

He texted back immediately with a thumbs up emoji. *R U in line?*

No, across the street.

Minutes later MJ appeared at the passenger-side window of my car. "How come you came to pick me up?" he asked as he hopped in. He usually walked from his school to the bus stop, then rode the city bus to my office.

"I was in the neighborhood. Hungry?"

MJ smiled and we both laughed. MJ had never answered that question with anything but an affirmative response. "In-N-Out okay?"

"Hell, yeah."

The In-N-Out parking lot was full, as usual, so I joined the drive-through line. While we inched forward, I asked MJ about his day, his classes, Sofia, Tim and Richard, and baby Aaron. I received the usual combination of "fine," "I dunno," and shoulder shrug. Then I asked, "How's your uncle?"

That elicited raised eyebrows. "Uncle Alex?"

"Do you have any other uncles?"

"He's okay, I guess. Why you asking?"

I shrugged as if it was no big deal. "I was thinking of paying him a visit." I knew if I tried to talk to Alex over the phone about what I'd found on the flash drive, he'd shut me down. And if I texted him a photo, he'd kill me.

"In LA?" MJ asked.

"Isn't that where he lives?"

"Yeah, but you better call first. He doesn't like it when people just show up at his place. My mom did that once, and he got really mad."

Of course, I would call first. I had to. I didn't know Alex's address. But even if I could pry it out of MJ, I'd still call first. I didn't want to accidentally walk in on something I shouldn't. "Can you call him or text him and ask when would be a good time for me to come?"

"Sure," MJ said, pulling his phone out of his pocket. "But why don't you just do it yourself?"

I gave him the same nonchalant shrug. "I don't know. Last time he wanted you to call me, so I figured I should return the favor." I didn't know if Alex had a reason for not calling me directly, but just in case, I wanted to follow his protocol.

"You guys are cray-cray," MJ said as he thumbed his screen.

"I know. It's a grownup thing."

INSTEAD OF GOING to the office after lunch, I drove MJ back to Tim and Richard's house.

"No work today?" he asked.

"Let's take the afternoon off." I was too exhausted to be productive and I was yearning to see baby Aaron again.

"You look like hell," Tim said when I walked into the kitchen behind MJ.

"You're not looking so great yourself," I replied, and we both laughed, although it wasn't true. Tim did look good or, at least, better than the last time I'd seen him. He still looked tired, but his clothes and hair were clean, and baby Aaron was strapped to his chest. He wasn't in a Baby Bjorn like Jonah used to use with Amelia. This was one of those complicated cotton wraps that held the baby curled up and facing in, so all I could see of Aaron was the side of his face.

I rubbed the side of Aaron's cheek—his skin was so soft—and said, "I broke up with Daniel last night."

"Oh no," Tim cried. "What happened?"

I shook my head. "I'm too tired to explain. I'm going home to take a nap, otherwise I'd offer to watch this cutie for you. But don't worry, we're still on for Saturday." I'd offered to babysit and planned on bringing Daniel with me. Now I'd be babysitting alone.

"I wasn't worried about Saturday. I'm worried about you."

"I'm fine." Or at least I would be after I got some sleep.

When I arrived at Tim and Richard's house Saturday afternoon, I was surprised to see Alex's BMW parked out front. I knew he was driving up that morning to take MJ and Sofia to see Maria, but I thought the plan had been for him to meet me at my house later in the evening after I finished babysitting. At least, that's what MJ, who was acting as our messenger, told me.

I knocked lightly on the front door, but the dogs heard me and started barking. Tim shushed them as he ushered me in, but it was too late. I heard Aaron wailing from upstairs.

"Damn dogs," Tim muttered. "I just got him down for a nap."

"Sorry. I should've texted to let you know I was here."

"It wouldn't have mattered," Tim said. "They bark every time I open the door these days. I think they've gotten louder since we brought Aaron home."

I laughed and bent down to pet Molly, a Chihuahua who couldn't have weighed more than ten pounds, and Vixen, a long-haired mutt who was three times Molly's size. "You wouldn't have barked at me, would you?"

Vixen licked my face and Molly jumped on me. Then Aaron let out another wail, which the dogs countered with more barking. Tim dropped his head and mumbled, "Please god, give me strength."

"I'll get him," I said and ran up the steps. I waved at Sofia, Makeyla, and Ethan, who were playing in the girls' bedroom, and followed the sound of the crying into Tim and Richard's bedroom, which I realized I'd never been inside before. Most of it was tastefully decorated with dark wood furniture and gray linens, which made the stark white bassinet and changing table stand out even more.

I changed Aaron's diaper, which was wet, then brought him downstairs to the living room where Tim, Richard, and Alex were seated in silence. When I walked in, all three men looked at me.

It was Tim who spoke. "I believe you know MJ's uncle."

"Yes," I replied and faced Alex. "Weren't we supposed to meet later?"

"Change of plans," he said.

I waited for an explanation, but he didn't offer one, so I turned back to Tim and Richard. "You guys can go. Aaron and I will be fine."

"I need to feed him first," Tim replied and reached out for the baby.

I held onto Aaron. "I know how to feed a baby, Tim."

"She does," Richard said.

"Then I'll just make his bottle," Tim replied.

And before I could tell him I knew how to do that too, he'd jumped up from the couch and was headed into the kitchen.

Richard shook his head.

"Don't worry," I said. "He'll be fine."

"Which one?" he asked, and we both laughed.

I carried Aaron into the kitchen where Tim was mixing his bottle. "I can do that, you know."

"I know," he said, shaking the container.

I was about to ask him if everything was okay when Richard and Alex appeared next to me, looking as uncomfortable together in the kitchen as they had been in the living room. "Ready to go?" Richard asked.

Tim handed me the bottle and said, "Give me a minute to change my shirt," before he ran upstairs.

I placed the bottle in Aaron's mouth, and he sucked on it greedily, oblivious to the tension in the room. "Where are you guys going?" I asked.

"Movies," Richard replied. "Then maybe we'll get a bite to eat. Don't worry though, we'll be back early."

I wasn't worried. Now that Daniel and I had broken up, I had no plans for my evening other than seeing Alex and he was already here. I thought I might miss Daniel a little, but I didn't. All I missed was the sex. Aside from that, it was a relief not to have to deal with him anymore.

"What movie are you going to see?" I asked just to keep the conversation going.

"Whatever starts in the next half hour and has lots of action. It's the only way I'll stay awake."

Alex chuckled. "The new *Fast and Furious* isn't bad."

Richard grinned. "I love those films."

"Why?" I asked. "There's no story. It's just car chases."

"Exactly," Richard said, then he and Alex both laughed.

Tim appeared at the bottom of the staircase, his stained T-shirt replaced by a clean button-down. "What's so funny?"

I said, "You're going to see the new *Fast and Furious* film."

"Really?" He turned to Richard. "But there's no story. It's just car chases."

Richard and Alex burst out laughing again, and Tim turned to me with a quizzical expression. *Go with it*, I mouthed.

Tim kissed both Aaron and me on the top of the head and said, "MJ and Isaiah are playing basketball at the park, but they know they need to be home before dark. Ethan and the girls are upstairs." Then he and Richard called out their goodbyes to the kids and were gone.

Alex, Aaron, and I were on our own.

Chapter 27

WHEN AARON FINISHED HIS BOTTLE, I tried to set him down on his play mat, but he cried. He also cried when I held him on my lap. He only stopped crying when I bounced him in my arms while I walked in circles around the living room. Alex seemed amused by my attempts to keep Aaron entertained. At least, he was smiling more than usual.

"Would you like a turn?" I asked.

"Nope," he said and folded his arms across his chest. "What did you want to talk to me about?"

"Don't you think we should wait until we're alone?"

Alex nodded to the baby. "You think he's gonna talk?"

I laughed. "Point taken. I figured out the password to the flash drive."

Alex's expression remained inscrutable.

"Don't you want to know what's on it?" I asked.

"Nope."

"Really? You're not even a little bit curious?"

"Curiosity killed the cat."

"I'm not a cat."

"That doesn't mean you can't be killed."

It sounded like a stampede of elephants barreling down the stairs, but it was only Sofia, Makeyla, and Ethan. The three huddled together at the entrance to the living room, then Sofia stepped in front of the other two, obviously the group's spokesperson. "Can we have ice cream?"

She'd directed her question to me, so I answered. "Is there any in the freezer?" I didn't think Tim and Richard kept ice cream in the house.

"No, but the ice cream man's at the park."

I didn't know if they were tracking the ice cream man on an app or just guessing, but I didn't care. I was tired of walking around the living room in circles and would rather be outside. Fresh air would be better for Aaron too. "Sure. Get your shoes on."

The kids thundered back up the staircase and I turned to Alex, who was doing a poor job of hiding his smile. "What? You got a problem with ice cream in the middle of the day?"

"Nope."

"Good," I said then I searched all the rooms downstairs until I found Tim's baby wrap in the hall closet.

When I returned to the living room, Alex and the kids were waiting for me. "Arms out," I said to Alex.

"Why?" he asked.

I handed Aaron to Makeyla and held up the baby carrier.

"You want to wrap me like a mummy?" Alex asked.

"It's for the baby. So you can carry him."

He shook his head. "No way."

"Why not?" I asked.

"You wear it," he said.

"Those things hurt my back." Jonah was the one who used to wear Amelia in the baby carrier. I always walked with her in the carriage.

"Don't they have a stroller?" Alex said.

Yes, it was parked in the dining room. But there was no way I was using it to get to the park. This neighborhood was filled with huge trees that had been planted decades ago. Between the giant roots stretching out everywhere and the earthquake damage that had never been repaired, the sidewalks were badly buckled. And I didn't want to attempt to navigate their busy street with three rambunctious kids and a baby carriage. I held up the carrier again. "C'mon, just try it."

Alex didn't move.

"You know," I said in what I hoped was a sultry voice, "there's nothing sexier than a man with a baby."

All three kids laughed. Even Alex cracked a smile. "Is that a fact?"

"Actually, it is," I told him. "Scientific studies have proven women find men with babies sexier than men without babies. It's a survival of the species thing. Google it if you don't believe me."

Alex sighed. "Can't you just hold him?"

"Yeah, but they start to get really heavy after a while. C'mon, just try it. Tim loves this thing. My husband loved ours too. If you hate it, you can take it off and we'll take turns holding him."

Alex grumbled but agreed. The wrap style baby carriers were much more complicated to use than the backpack style Jonah preferred. But with the help of a YouTube video, we figured it out.

"You look good, Uncle A," Sofia said when Aaron was strapped to his chest.

"Yeah, Uncle A," I said. "*Very* sexy."

The kids laughed. Alex didn't. He grumbled and said, "Let's go before I change my mind."

The three kids walked ahead of us, but they were still close enough to hear and I didn't want to talk about the flash drive in front of them. So I asked Alex about his visit with Maria.

"They're kicking her out."

"Why? I thought she was doing really well." That's what MJ told me.

"They're transitioning her to a halfway house," he said.

"That's good, isn't it?" I didn't know much about halfway houses, but it sounded like a positive step.

"If she stays clean it is. If not, she goes back to jail."

"Fingers crossed for her then."

Alex snorted loudly and Aaron squawked, then his eyelids began to droop again.

"I think he likes you," I said. "He looks very content."

"He likes movement. If we drove him in the car, he'd be just as happy."

He sounded like a man who'd taken care of a baby. "Do you have kids?" I'd never thought to ask before. Although if MJ and Sofia had first cousins, it seemed like one of them would've mentioned it by now.

"No."

"Or none that you know of."

"None, period."

"You can't know that for sure," I said.

Alex stared at me with his dark eyes, a slight smile around his lips. "Why so interested?"

I could feel the heat rising in my cheeks and looked away. The scientists were right. Alex did look more attractive with a baby strapped to his chest. "Just making conversation."

Alex grinned and patted the baby carrier. "Maybe I *should* get myself one of these." We continued walking in silence, listening to the kids argue over whether the live action or animated Spider Man was best, when Alex said, "Do you want another kid?"

"You mean have another child?" I asked.

"Yes."

I shrugged. "I don't know. Maybe."

"You should. You're a good mom."

I let out a laugh. "I don't know about that. Feeding kids ice cream in the middle of the day? I think they kick you out of the Good Mommy Club for that." I could think of several mothers from the Mommy & Me group I used to take Amelia to who would be appalled at how much junk food I let MJ and Sofia consume.

Alex didn't laugh. He sounded angry. "You're a better mother to those kids than Maria ever was. They should be living with you, not the gays."

I let the slur pass without comment because I didn't want to have that argument in front of the kids. "You know that's not possible."

"No. Why isn't it possible?"

I stared at Alex. I'd assumed MJ had told him the reason, but maybe not. I lowered my voice so the kids wouldn't hear and said, "Because according to the State of California, I'm not currently fit to be a parent."

"*You're* not fit to be a parent?" he said incredulously. "What'd you do? Kill a puppy?"

"No, I did not kill a puppy! How could you even think such a thing?"

"Well, you must've done something pretty bad, if they think you're unfit. And I didn't say you killed the dog on purpose. I was thinking maybe you ran it over with your car."

"No, I did not run over a puppy."

"Then what did you do?"

I lowered my voice again. "I attempted suicide. I was unsuccessful. Obviously."

"Oh," Alex said, then stared straight ahead over the top of Aaron's fuzzy scalp.

"It happened before I met MJ," I continued. "That's why Aunt Maddy had to be the kids' foster parent instead of me. The State won't let me."

We were silent for the rest of the walk to the park. When we were still half a block away the kids heard the ice cream man's bell and they raced ahead. I ran to catch up with them, leaving Alex and Aaron behind.

I paid for Sofia's strawberry popsicle, Ethan's chocolate covered cone, and Makeyla's ice cream sandwich and accompanied them to a low cement wall where a group of other children congregated eating their own ice creams.

When Alex arrived a few minutes later he asked me if I wanted ice cream too. I didn't, and neither did he. Then I glanced around the playground and spotted a bench a couple with a squirmy toddler had just vacated. I hustled over to it before another parent could snag it and motioned for Alex to join me. He sat down on the opposite end, his legs spread wide, a sleeping Aaron resting between them.

I said, "The reason I wanted to talk to you again is because I need your help."

Chapter 28

ALEX DIDN'T RESPOND. He continued to stare straight ahead, pretending to watch the kids playing on the climbing structure.

"Don't you want to know what I need your help with?" I asked.

"No."

"It has to do with the flash drive," I said, undeterred.

Alex blew air out his nose and gripped the bench. "I told you to get rid of it."

"No, you told me to get it out of the house. At least, that's the message MJ gave me. And I did. It's somewhere safe."

"Where?"

"The bank. I put it in my safe deposit box."

Alex laughed.

"What's so funny?"

He shook his head but didn't reply.

"Can I please tell you what I found on it?"

"I think you're going to tell me anyway."

He was right about that. "I'd rather show you."

"You're gonna sneak me into the bank and take me to your safe deposit box?" He laughed again.

I didn't get the humor in safe deposit boxes, but obviously he did. "No, I downloaded the file onto my laptop."

Alex stopped laughing and turned to face me. "Are you fucking kidding me? What the fuck were you thinking?"

Aaron stirred but didn't wake. However, the half dozen parents within earshot turned and stared at us. "Keep your voice down," I hissed.

"Keep my voice down?" He lowered his volume but not his angry tone.

I smiled for the benefit of the parents who were still giving us sidelong glances. "C'mon, let's take a walk."

I stood up, but Alex stayed seated, silently fuming. I left him on the bench while I ran over to the kids. I told them not to leave the playground area until we returned. When all three had promised, I walked back to the bench and stared at Alex with my hands on my hips until he stood up.

"I feel like you're always mad at me," I said as we strode side by side along the cement path that led to the soccer field.

"When I tell you to get something out of your house, it means get it away from you, not transfer it to your goddamn computer."

"I can count on one hand the number of people who even know the flash drive exists."

Alex stopped in the middle of the path. "Wrong! You have no idea who knows about the flash drive or why they might want it."

I took a deep breath and let it out slowly. Fighting with Alex was not going to get him to help me. "Actually, I think I might know or, at least, why someone would want it. There's only one file on the drive. A spreadsheet. I think it might be a list of private keys. Do you know what those are? They're—"

"I know what a private key is!" Alex said, shaking his head in disgust.

"Enough, Alex." I wouldn't put up with Daniel's condescension and I wasn't going to accept it from Alex either. "I apologize if I insulted you. It wasn't my intention. Now stop insulting me. I had no idea what a private key was until my ex told me."

"Your ex?"

"Just someone I dated for a few weeks."

"The math teacher?"

Obviously, MJ had told him about Daniel, although I didn't know why. "Yes, but we broke up."

"Why?"

"Does it matter?"

"You want my help, don't you?"

I let out another slow breath and reminded myself again that I didn't just want Alex's help, I needed it. I had no one else to turn to. "If you must know, it's because he thinks I'm crazy."

Alex let out a laugh and Aaron stirred. "You are crazy," he said and resumed walking.

"Not crazy the way you think I'm crazy. Tinfoil hat crazy. Check myself into the Wellstone Center crazy."

"Why? What did you do?"

"I told him I thought the file on the flash drive might have something to do with why Jonah and Amelia were killed."

Alex didn't respond. He stared straight ahead and kept walking.

"Do you agree? Or do you think I'm tinfoil hat crazy too?"

"That depends."

"On?"

Alex stopped and turned to face me. "What you're planning to do with the file."

"Well, I wasn't going to steal anyone's crypto if that's what you're thinking."

"I wasn't."

"That's why I need your help. I don't know anything about

this stuff. If the file really is a list of private keys, how do I find the owners?"

"You don't," he said and started walking again.

"You don't understand. That's my—"

Alex stopped short and pointed his finger in my face. "No, *you* don't understand. You need to delete that file and move on with your life."

"I can't delete it and move on with my life! What if those private keys are somehow connected to my family's murder?"

"What if they are? Knowing won't bring them back."

"But if I know what the connection is, I could go to the police."

"What do you think the police are gonna do?"

"Arrest them."

"The shooter is dead. The police don't arrest dead men."

"But I still don't know *why* he shot them. And I need to. Not knowing will kill me."

"Wrong," he said, pointing his finger in my face again. "It's the people who own those private keys who'll kill you."

I sucked in my breath. "You know who they are?"

"I didn't say that."

"You must know or, at least, have an idea, if you're so sure they're going to kill me."

Alex shook his head. "Go ask your brother-in-law."

"If Jake knew, those people would be dead already."

"Maybe they are."

"Enough with the riddles, Alex. Tell me what you know."

"What I know is pursuing these people will not bring your family back. All it will do is get you killed too."

"That's a risk I'm willing to take."

"Well, I'm not." Alex yanked Aaron out of the baby carrier and shoved him into my chest. Not surprisingly, Aaron began to wail. I tried to quiet him while Alex attempted to free himself from the baby carrier, but he got so frustrated with the complicated knot that he pulled a pocketknife out of his jeans and sliced through the fabric instead. The cotton wrapping fell to the ground in pieces.

"I can't believe you just did that," I said, staring at the shredded baby carrier. Aaron was stunned silent for a moment too then started to bawl again. I rubbed circles on his back to try to calm him down as I shouted at Alex, who was walking away from us. "I'm going to find out the truth with or without your help."

"Then stay away from my niece and nephew," he called over his shoulder. "They don't need to mourn your death too."

Chapter 29

JANELLE WAS at the office when I arrived late Monday morning. "I was wondering if you were coming in today."

I dropped my briefcase and purse onto my desk and stuck my head in her office. "Sorry, did we have something scheduled? I didn't see anything on my calendar."

I almost hadn't come in at all. I'd had to force myself to shower and leave the house today. It had been months since I'd felt this way. But since the fight with Alex on Saturday, I could feel myself slipping back into depression. I'd been elated when I'd finally cracked the password on Jonah's flash drive, but now I wished I'd never found the damn thing. No one but Alex believed it had something to do with Jonah and Amelia's death, and he refused to help. I had nowhere left to turn.

"No," Janelle replied, bringing me back to the present. "I was just hoping to talk to you before I had to leave for court. Do you have a minute?"

"Sure," I said, and flopped down onto her guest chair. "What's up?"

"A couple things. First, they're moving Maria to a halfway house later this week. I thought you'd want to know."

"I heard," I said. "Alex told me."

"You still keep in touch with him?" She seemed surprised.

I was not going to explain to Janelle why Alex and I were speaking again. Although after Saturday I wasn't sure if we were speaking anymore. "He took the kids to visit Maria this weekend."

Janelle nodded. "Her lawyer called this morning. She's petitioning to regain custody."

That wasn't a surprise. We all assumed she would. "You think they'll give it to her?"

"Not right away. She'll have to get a job first, a new apartment, submit to weekly drug testing. But in the meantime, the judge will likely grant her supervised visits. That's where you come in."

"Me?"

"I talked to MJ's foster dad this morning. He told me they have a new baby—"

I nodded. "Aaron. I know."

"He told me they're a bit overwhelmed at the moment so they couldn't commit to supervising the kids' visits with Maria, but he suggested you might be able to."

I was surprised Tim hadn't asked me first. Although we both knew I had the time. I just wasn't sure I was the right person for the job. "I doubt Maria will want me there."

"Maria doesn't get to choose," Janelle said. "The question is are you willing? If not, I'll have to find an alternative. Maybe a group setting."

I didn't like the sound of *group setting*. I didn't think a Mommy and Me class was what Janelle had in mind. "I'll do it as long as Maria's okay with it."

"Like I said, Maria has no say in this."

"Then I guess it's settled. Was that all?" I didn't have

anywhere I needed to be, I just preferred to wallow in sadness alone.

"No," Janelle said. "Next week will be six months since we started working together."

"Has it been six months already?" It didn't feel like six months. Maybe half that.

"We said when we started, we'd give it six months and then decide."

I glanced around the office taking in the mostly bare walls and acoustic ceiling tiles. We could paint and add some artwork, but there was no disguising this place was a strip mall office. "I'm not opposed to moving if you'd rather somewhere nicer."

"Actually, Grace, I've accepted an offer from another firm."

"Oh," I said and my heart started racing. I wasn't expecting that. I'd thought our arrangement was working. Janelle got to keep the cases she liked and hand off all the clients she didn't want to deal with to me. I can't say I loved the work, but I didn't hate it either. Once Janelle taught me the basics, the job became very routine. But every once in a while I felt like I was making a positive difference in someone's life, and that was enough for now. I also liked setting my own hours and not having a boss. Maybe that's what Janelle didn't like about our arrangement. She was used to having an associate working for her rather than a partner with whom she shared space.

"It's nothing personal," Janelle said. "I wasn't looking to leave. The firm approached me, and it just seemed like the right move, professionally."

"Of course," I said, trying to keep the hurt out of my voice. "Which firm?"

"Cadawaler Erickson."

"I thought you hated them. Didn't they poach your former associate?"

Janelle smiled. "Good memory. They just merged with a

national firm, and she reached out. They're under a lot of pressure to increase their diversity."

"And you're okay with that?" Janelle had made derogatory comments before about big companies allegedly embracing diversity without ever changing their ways.

"I'm okay with the salary they offered. I'm tired of always feeling like I'm teetering on the edge. I can talk to them about bringing you in too if you want. Maybe as of counsel or something."

We both knew if the firm was looking to increase their diversity, they wouldn't be interested in hiring me. They had enough white lawyers. "Thanks, but I don't want to go back to a big firm."

"You sure? Because I don't think I'm going to be able to hand off any clients to you once I leave. They've already got plenty of lawyers to handle those types of clients."

"Yes, but thank you for the offer."

"What will you do?" Janelle asked. "Are you going to stay here? Try to build up your own practice?"

Honestly, I had no idea.

Chapter 30

I WAITED for Janelle to leave for court before I left the office too. I went straight home, changed into sweatpants, and spent the rest of the day laying on the couch daydreaming about Before, crying about After, and generally feeling sorry for myself. I forgot I was supposed to go to my aunt's house for dinner tonight. If I remembered, I would've cancelled.

The house was dark when my aunt unlocked the front door with her spare key and let herself in. She flipped on the lights and spotted me curled up on the couch. I could see she was relieved but angry too.

"Are we back to this again?" she said, joining me in the living room.

"Please go," I replied and rolled over so she couldn't see my tear-stained face.

She sat down on the chair closest to me. "When I couldn't reach you, I tried MJ. At least, he answers his phone."

"I forgot we had plans. I'm sorry."

"He told me Janelle took another job. Is that what this is about?"

"No."

"Then what?" she asked.

I didn't reply. Maybe if I didn't answer she'd leave. I just wanted to be alone with my misery.

"Have you talked to Dr. Rubenstein?"

"No," I mumbled. "We're taking a break." I'd made the decision after our last session. I didn't want a therapist who didn't believe me.

"Do you think that's wise?"

When I didn't answer, Aunt Maddy smooshed in next to me on the couch and pulled one of my hands out from under the blanket. "Talk to me, sweetie. I know the grief can come out of nowhere sometimes, but did something happen to set you off?"

I nodded and sprouted fresh tears.

"Please tell me."

So I did. I thought Aunt Maddy would think I'm crazy too. But if she did, she didn't say so. She went into the kitchen and returned with two small glasses of white wine. The leftover from Daniel's last visit I presumed. I sat upright but didn't drink. "I don't think you're supposed to have alcohol when you're depressed. It only makes it worse." They'd told us that at the Wellstone Center.

"You're right," she said and poured the wine from my glass into hers.

"What do you think?" I asked as she sipped her drink.

She sighed. "I don't know what to think."

"Can you honestly tell me all these things are just random coincidences? That I'm deluding myself because I can't accept that sometimes bad things really do happen to good people?" I'd heard many platitudes since Jonah and Amelia's death, but that one annoyed me the most.

She set her wineglass down on the coffee table. "No. Even at the time I thought it was odd that the police never investigated."

That jolted me. "Why am I first hearing about this now? If you were suspicious back then, why didn't you say something?"

"I didn't say I was suspicious. I just thought it all seemed a bit...tidy. The police get an anonymous tip, the suspect pulls a gun, the police shoot him dead. Case closed. That does happen sometimes. It's not necessarily a sign something nefarious is going on."

"But?"

"It's convenient too." She picked up her glass and swirled the wine absentmindedly. "Although even if I had been suspicious back then, I'm not sure I would've said anything."

"Why not?"

"You were a wreck, Grace. You didn't sleep, you didn't eat, some days you wouldn't even get out of bed. There's no way I would've said or done anything to prolong your suffering."

It wouldn't have prolonged my suffering; it would've eased it. It would've given me something to focus on besides my grief. But I didn't say that. Instead, I asked, "And now?"

"Now," she sighed and shook her head. "I can't even believe I'm saying this, but I'm siding with the drug dealer."

"You think Alex is right? That I should just delete the file and move on with my life?"

"I do."

"I can't do that. You *know* I can't do that. It will eat at me for the rest of my life."

"Nothing you uncover will bring Jonah and Amelia back. And if it's justice you're after, well, the shooter's dead."

"But what if he wasn't acting alone? What if other people are involved and they're still out there living their life while my family's gone?"

"If they're out there, they won't want to be found. I think that's why Alex was trying to warn you."

"I know he knows something, but he won't tell me. He told me to go ask Jake."

"What if," Aunt Maddy said, "and God forgive me for even thinking this, Jake is somehow involved? Do you really want to stir up that hornet's nest?"

I had no idea what I would do if I found out Jake was somehow responsible for Jonah and Amelia's death. I couldn't even let my mind go there.

"Think, Grace," she continued. "What good could possibly come from pursuing this? Alex is right. You need to let this go."

AUNT MADDY SPENT the night at my house. I'd suggested it because she'd drunk a lot of wine. She agreed because she didn't trust me not to do something stupid, even though I told her I was feeling better.

Over coffee and toast the next morning, Aunt Maddy asked if I'd given any more thought to what she'd said.

"That's all I've thought about." I hadn't slept much, which was evident from the dark circles under my eyes.

"And?" she asked.

Chapter 31

I felt like I was back where I'd started. Once Maria regained custody of MJ and Sofia, I might never see them again. I was about to be unemployed. Again. I was alone. Again. And I was no closer to knowing whether Jonah and Amelia's deaths were random bad luck or a targeted killing.

No, you know.

Yes, I know. I may not have proof, but I know.

I stared at my aunt across the kitchen table. "You know I can't let this go."

She hung her head and sighed. "I was hoping to be wrong this time."

I smiled. "Sorry, but you know me too well."

"If I can't convince you not to do this, can I at least offer you some advice?"

"Please. You know much more about criminals than I do." She'd won a Pulitzer for her investigative reporting on a Miami crime syndicate. "Where do I start?"

"*Not* with the criminals. That's the quickest way to get yourself killed. Start with Jake."

"You honestly think Jake will tell me the truth?"

"Not if he's mixed up in this. But that doesn't mean you can't get information out of him."

"And how do you suggest I do that? He wouldn't even tell me why he was at my house that day."

"You're a smart girl, Grace. I'm sure you'll figure something out."

Chapter 32

I waited for Jake in the bar of the Mexican restaurant. He was surprised when I'd called since we hadn't spoken in several months, but he readily agreed to meet me for dinner tonight. I chose this restaurant because it was close to Jake's apartment. Jonah and I had eaten there with Jake once and I knew Jake liked the place. I liked that I could park my car one block over from Jake's apartment and walk to the restaurant. My plan could've worked if we had two cars, but it would be easier with one.

I assumed the bar would be crowded on a Friday night and it was. But I came early and saved us two seats. I spent the extra time sipping my virgin margarita and rehearsing my story in my head. I spotted Jake first and, as usually happened since Jonah's death, the sight of him took my breath away. His face was so similar to Jonah's that I felt like I was looking at a ghost. It took me a moment to reorient my thinking and focus on their differences. Jake was taller and broader than Jonah, and he walked with a swagger that Jonah never had.

Would Jonah approve of what I was about to do to his brother? The answer would depend on whether his loyalties laid with Jake or with me. Before Jonah died, I would've said his loyalties laid with me. I was his wife and the mother of his child. But now I wasn't so sure.

I hopped off my barstool and hugged Jake and he planted a kiss on my cheek.

"You started without me," he said, nodding at my drink.

"My meeting finished early." I had to shout to be heard over the bar's din. Everyone was cheering because the Dodgers had just scored in the game playing on the big screen TV. "You'll need two just to catch up to me."

His eyebrows shot up. "Are we celebrating?"

I shook my head. "The opposite."

I'd prepared a story about why I was in LA for the day—I'd lost a big custody dispute and had to drive my client down to her father's house in Manhattan Beach—but Jake never asked. He said, "Then let's get you drunk," which was exactly the response I'd been hoping for.

I hopped back up onto my barstool and moved my purse off the seat next to mine so Jake could sit down. He flagged down the bartender and ordered a margarita for himself and turned to me.

"And a shot of tequila," I told the bartender.

"You must really be having a bad day if you're drinking shots."

"It's not for me, it's for you. So you can catch up."

Jake smiled. "Challenge accepted."

Jake didn't bring up the last time we'd seen each other and neither did I. We kept the conversation superficial—his work, my work, good movies we'd seen. Jake kept half his attention on me and the other half on the baseball game playing on the TV above my head, which was fine with me.

I concentrated on sucking down my virgin margaritas as quickly as I could then ordering "the same" from the bartender.

Each time I ordered another drink, Jake did too. Jake wasn't just competitive with Jonah. He was competitive with everyone about everything, a fact I'd been counting on. When he excused himself to use the men's room, I took the opportunity to order two more shots, both of which I dumped into his glass before he returned. I figured by that point he was drunk enough not to notice. I was right.

When Jake started yelling at the television because he disagreed with the umpire's call, the bartender told him he'd have to cut him off.

"Who the fuck do you think you are?" Jake shouted.

I knew that was our cue to leave. I placed my hand on Jake's arm, forcing his attention to me. "Let's go back to your place. It'll be quieter and you can drink whatever you want."

Jake glanced from me to the bartender, a soft-spoken older gentleman who was definitely not looking for a fight. "Sure," he said, "Let's get out of here."

I paid our tab and left the bartender a generous tip. "For your discretion," I said.

The bartender nodded at Jake. "Do you need help?"

"No, I'm good, thanks."

When the valet pulled up in Jonah's Audi—I still thought of it as Jonah's even after all this time—Jake tried to get in behind the wheel. The valet helped me steer Jake around to the passenger side and buckle him into the seat.

"How come you can drive?" Jake asked as I pulled out onto the street.

"I paced myself." He was drunk enough to accept my explanation.

JAKE'S APARTMENT looked exactly as I remembered it—leather furniture, giant flat-screen television, and paper everywhere.

Jake obviously still preferred to read in print form. Old newspapers and magazines were piled up on every available surface, along with stacks of manila folders.

"You want a drink?" Jake asked.

I didn't think he'd let me make the cocktails, so I said, "Just water for me."

"C'mon, have a beer with me."

"I don't want to mix."

"Liquor then beer, never fear!"

I laughed. It had been years since anyone had used that line on me. "Okay, but just one. I still need to drive back to Santa Veneta tonight." I was supervising Maria's visit with MJ and Sofia the next morning. I didn't need to pick up the kids until eleven, so I could've spent the night at Jake's and driven home early the next morning if I wanted to. But I didn't want to. I wanted to get the answers to my questions as quickly as possible then leave.

Jake handed me a beer, and I followed him into the living room. He was still upright but swaying.

"Sorry about the mess," he said, collapsing onto the couch. "I wasn't expecting company."

"I'm not company," I said. "I'm family."

"Are we still family?"

Technically, no, but I said, "I think so. Don't you?"

He nodded, and I knew his thoughts had turned to Jonah because his smile disappeared. "Drink," he said and clinked his beer bottle against mine.

I took a small sip and set my beer down on the coffee table. Jake drained a few inches from his beer and held onto the bottle. "Do you still miss him?" he asked.

"There's not a day that goes by that I don't miss both of them. I don't think that ever goes away."

Jake nodded. "Same."

I knew this was my opening. Jake had avoided talking about Jonah all evening. Every time I'd tried to bring him up, Jake would change the subject or focus his attention on the baseball game. "Do you ever wish there had been a trial?" I asked.

Jake turned to me. "For who?"

"The guy who shot them. We don't know anything about him. The police never investigated."

"What is there to investigate? The guy was crazy, probably hopped up on something. I'm glad the cops shot him."

I knew I didn't have long. Jake's eyelids were drooping. "But don't you think they should've arrested him? I mean, that's how the system's supposed to work. The police aren't supposed to just execute people."

Jake's head lolled backwards but his voice was still angry. "Don't you dare give me the innocent until proven guilty speech. That fucker murdered my brother. I would've shot him myself if I could." Jake drained the rest of his beer. He attempted to place the empty bottle on the coffee table, but he missed and it landed on the rug.

I grabbed his bottle off the floor and set it down on the coffee table next to mine. "I just wish I knew what drove him to do what he did."

Jake let out a harsh laugh. "What drove him? He's a fucking criminal, Grace. That's what criminals do."

"But was he always a criminal? I mean, he wasn't born a murderer. What made him that way?"

"Are you fucking kidding me? The guy gunned down your family and you want to know if his mother hugged him enough when he was a kid?"

"Yes! Why would someone do that, Jake? He didn't know Jonah. He had no beef with him."

"The guy was a sociopath. He had a rap sheet a mile long.

Armed robbery, assault, possession." He counted them off on his fingers. "Murdered plenty of people too, just never got caught."

"How do you know all that? Did the police tell you? Because they never told me."

Jake grinned. "I told them."

And there it was. Finally. A nugget of truth. "But how did you know? Did you have one of your FBI friends look him up in some database or something?"

"Or something." Jake leaned his head back and placed his forearm over his eyes, shielding them from the overhead light. "I told the local cops where to find him."

"They told me they got an anonymous tip."

"They did. From me."

Neither of us spoke after that. Jake because he fell asleep, and me because even though I'd orchestrated this whole evening because I'd wanted information, now that I had answers, I was stunned. I continued to believe Amelia's death was an accident mainly because I didn't want to believe that anyone, even a sociopath, would intentionally murder an innocent child. But Jonah's death wasn't an accident. I felt sure of that now, even though I still didn't know why anyone would want to kill him.

I would've asked Jake more questions, but he was passed out. I couldn't even rouse him long enough to get him into his bed, so I just rolled him over onto his side in case he got sick during the night and left him on the couch.

I considered driving back to Santa Veneta then. In hindsight, I should have. But I had no way of knowing my luck was about to run out.

Chapter 33

I KNEW I'd never be able to leave everything in Jake's apartment exactly where I'd found it, so I decided to clean it instead. That way everything would be out of place and Jake wouldn't be suspicious. I tossed our beer bottles into the bin then returned to the living room to tackle the mountains of paper. I was afraid to throw anything in the trash in case Jake was saving it for some reason, so I sorted all the newspapers and magazines into neat piles and stacked them on the coffee table.

In the process I uncovered several printed articles explaining how to grade diamonds along with a jeweler's loop, which surprised me. Was Jake planning on buying someone an engagement ring? When I'd asked him if he was dating anyone, he'd told me no one special.

After I'd sorted the papers near the couch and TV, I moved to Jake's desk, which was in the corner of the living room. It was cheap particleboard, probably from Ikea, and matched the rest of the all-black furniture in the room. In the bottom drawer I found what I could only describe as dossiers. Each file contained information about an individual, always a man, usually but not always with a printed photo attached. The file also contained a bullet-pointed list that included the person's background, education, and family members. There was no company name or logo on the file folders, and none contained rap sheets, although a few of the dossiers noted time served for various crimes. If the men described in these files were white with eastern European sounding names, I would've concluded they were the Russian mobsters Alex had alluded to. But every one of them was Asian.

On top of the desk was a modem, a router, and a mouse, but no computer. I checked Jake's bedroom for his laptop, but all I found was an unmade bed and a pile of dirty laundry, along with photos of him, Jonah, and their mother. I recalled in the pre-Amelia days, whenever I used to meet someone for dinner or drinks after work, I always left my briefcase locked in the trunk of my car. I wondered if Jake did the same, then realized I didn't have to wonder because I still had access to his keys.

I snatched Jake's key ring from the kitchen counter where I'd set it atop a stack of unopened mail and headed downstairs to the parking garage. I found his laptop inside a messenger bag in his trunk along with more dossiers. I assumed the laptop was password-protected but checked to be sure. After a few failed attempts, I shut the computer. It had taken me months to guess Jonah's password. I would never be able to guess Jake's. But I wanted to read the dossiers and it was cold in the garage, so I stuffed everything into the messenger bag and headed back up to Jake's apartment.

I unlocked the front door and headed straight to the kitchen. I was afraid if I didn't return Jake's keys now while I was thinking about it, I would accidentally drive home with them. I placed the key ring on top of the unopened mail and turned to leave. That's when Jake appeared in front of me.

I screamed and jumped back, banging my head against a kitchen cabinet. "What are you doing?"

"I could ask you the same," he replied, eyeing his messenger bag, which was still slung over my shoulder, the top unzipped and the files sticking out the top.

"You were sleeping," I said as if that somehow explained my behavior.

"What are you doing with my bag?"

I said the first thing that popped into my throbbing head. "Well, I didn't think you'd want to leave it lying around in your car all night."

"It wasn't lying around in my car. It was locked in my trunk."

I had no defense. My only option was offense. "Yes, but I didn't know that until I got downstairs."

"And you thought since you were there anyway, you'd search my bag?"

I assumed that was a rhetorical question and didn't answer.

He yanked the messenger bag off my shoulder and rifled through it.

"I didn't steal anything if that's what you're worried about."

He finished searching then zipped the bag shut with the files tucked inside. "Why were you snooping through my things?"

I stayed with offense. "Why were you snooping through my house a few months ago?"

Jake's eyebrows raised. "Is that what this is about? Payback?"

"No. I just want answers. What were you and Jonah up to?"

"We weren't up to anything."

I gingerly touched the back of my head and felt the knot that was already forming. I was suddenly very tired. "Please, Jake. Just tell me why Jonah was killed."

"The shooter was mentally unstable. Probably high on drugs too."

"Stop lying! You told me he had a rap sheet, that he'd killed before, that you called in the anonymous tip."

"When?" he said, his anger matching my own.

"Earlier, before you fell asleep."

Jake stared at me slack jawed then asked, "Did you drug me?"

"No. You got drunk."

"I thought we both did, but you seem fine. What'd you do? Spill out all your drinks when I wasn't looking?"

I shook my head. "Virgin margaritas."

He folded his arms across his chest. "Well, aren't you clever."

I didn't respond.

"Wait here," Jake said pointing his finger at me. Then stomped off into his bedroom with the messenger bag.

I should've gone home. I wish I had. But I was distracted. How was Jake even awake? He was passed out when I left for the parking garage. And I made sure not to let the door slam shut when I let myself back in. Then I spotted the bottle of acetaminophen on the counter and the empty glass in the sink. He must've gotten up for aspirin while I was downstairs. He was probably in the bathroom when I snuck back in.

Jake reappeared without his messenger bag and headed straight to the refrigerator. He pulled out a can of Coke and split it between two glasses. He shoved one of the glasses into my hand and held up the other. "*Salud!*" he said and gulped down his soda. I took a sip from mine then said, "I should leave."

"No. You came here for answers, and you deserve them. Drink up."

I swigged my Coke and followed him into the living room.

He sat down on the couch and motioned for me to join him. I took a seat on the opposite end and waited for him to speak.

"Tell me everything you know," he said.

"How about you tell me everything you know?"

He sighed. "Grace, I'll tell you what I can, but when I keep things from you it's to protect you."

"Protect me from what?"

He didn't answer.

"The Russian mob?"

His eyebrows shot up, but he still said nothing.

"Does it have something to do with the flash drive?" I finally asked.

"What flash drive?"

"Isn't that what you were looking for at my house that day?"

And that's the last thing I remember.

Chapter 34

I OPENED my eyes and stared down at the weird stripes of light on the carpet, but my head ached so bad I shut them again. The next time I opened my eyes I realized those weird stripes of light were coming from the venetian blinds in Jake's living room. I rolled over onto my back and covered my eyes with my forearm. I had the worst hangover of my life. My entire head was pounding, and I thought I might vomit. I waited for the wave of nausea to pass before I opened my eyes again. I was fully clothed with a blanket covering me.

I forced myself upright and another wave of nausea hit. While I waited for it to pass, I heard someone moving around in the kitchen. I called out Jake's name and the effort forced me to lie down and close my eyes again.

"Sleep okay?" Jake asked.

I rolled over and was greeted by a pair of hairy legs. I looked up and saw the legs belonged to Jake. He was wearing gym shorts and a T-shirt and his hair was damp as if he'd just taken a shower.

Sleep okay? I could barely process the thought. "What happened?" I croaked.

"Don't you remember? We met for drinks, then came back to my place."

I sat up again. I remembered that part of the evening. It was after he found me with his messenger bag that was a blur. "Why do I have a hangover when I didn't drink?"

"You drank," he said. "We both did."

I shook my head and another wave of nausea crashed over me. "No. I only had a couple sips of beer."

"Let me get you some coffee," he said and returned to the kitchen.

I pushed myself upright and stumbled after him. The smell of the eggs he was frying smacked me in the face, and I barely made it to the kitchen sink before I started retching. Jake grabbed me, one arm around my ribcage and the other holding my hair back, while I vomited up everything left in my stomach. When I finished, I rinsed my mouth and splashed cold water on my face before I turned around.

"What did you do to me?" I asked, tears streaming down my face. I always cry when I vomit. I have since I was a kid.

"You'll be fine. It's no worse than a hangover." He reached for the bottle of acetaminophen, which was still out on the counter from the night before and shook two into his hand. He held them out to me with a glass of water. "Take them and go back to sleep. You'll feel better in a couple of hours."

I swatted his hand away and the pills skidded across the kitchen floor. "Did you drug me last night?"

"You drugged me too," he said unapologetically.

"No, I didn't. You got drunk all on your own."

"I thought I was keeping up with you. But it turns out you weren't drinking."

"So that justifies drugging me?"

He stared down at the kitchen floor.

"Jake, what did you do to me?" I could only think of one

reason to give someone a date rape drug, which is what I assumed he'd given me, although I didn't know for sure.

He must've read my mind because he said, "Not that! Jesus, Grace, I would never."

"Then why?"

"I needed to know how much you knew."

"You could've just asked me!"

"I did. But you wouldn't tell me unless I told you what I knew first, and I couldn't do that."

"Why?" I yelled, but the effort of holding myself upright with my head still throbbing was just too much for me. I sank down onto the kitchen floor and sobbed. Jake sat down next to me and placed his arm around my shoulder. I wanted to push him away, but I was too exhausted, and the scent of his freshly washed skin reminded me so much of Jonah I leaned my head against his shoulder and breathed him in.

When my tears subsided, Jake stood up and grabbed the bottle of acetaminophen off the counter. He held it out to me with a glass of water. "Take some. You'll feel better."

I swallowed down two tablets, then Jake pulled a can of Coke from the fridge and poured it into my now-empty glass. As soon as the bubbly, sugary liquid hit my stomach, it began to settle. I closed my eyes and leaned my head back against the kitchen cabinet. The knot at the back still hurt, but not as much as it had the night before.

Jake snatched another can of Coke from the fridge and joined me on the floor again. We sat together in silence until he finally said, "I'm sorry, Grace."

"Sorry for drugging me?"

"Sorry for everything."

Chapter 35

OF COURSE, I asked Jake what he meant by "everything." And of course, he refused to tell me.

"Someday I'll be able to explain," he said. "But not today."

"What does that even mean?"

"I can't tell you that either."

We went round and round in the same vein until the phone in his pocket started to buzz. He stood up to answer it and I leaned my head back and closed my eyes. I didn't pay much attention to Jake's side of the conversation until he said, "Yeah, she's right here." Then he held the phone out to me.

"Hello?"

"I'm buying you a new phone," Aunt Maddy said. "One you'll actually answer."

"Sorry, I must've left mine on vibrate." I pushed myself up from the kitchen floor and staggered back into the living room.

"We've been trying to reach you."

"Who's we?" I asked as I fished my phone out of my purse. Then I remembered I was supposed to be supervising MJ and Sofia's visit with Maria today. Shit. It was already ten-thirty. There was no way I could make it back to Santa Veneta in time.

"Where are you?" Aunt Maddy demanded.

"Jake's apartment." *Shouldn't she know that since we were talking on his phone? Although it was his cell, so we could be anywhere.*

"You slept over?"

"It's not what you think. Let me call you back. I need to call MJ and let him know I'm going to be late. I was supposed to take him and Sofia to see Maria today."

"I know. MJ called me when he couldn't reach you."

I checked my phone. I had a missed call and several texts from MJ. "Maybe Tim can do it this time."

"He can't. Aaron's sick."

"What's wrong? Is he okay?"

"Fever and a cough. They're waiting to hear back from the pediatrician."

I remembered the first time Amelia got sick. Jonah and I were so worried we both stayed up with her all night. Two days later she was fine. And three months after that they were both dead.

"Let me see if I can reschedule for later today. I can be back in two hours. Less if the traffic's light."

"Sofia has dance class at two."

"Since when?" I asked.

"Today. Makeyla moved out and Sofia's devastated. Apparently, the two were quite close. Tim signed her up for dance class, hoping she'll make a new friend."

"After dance class then." That would be better anyway since it would give me time to shower and change. My shirt both looked and smelled like it had been slept in.

"No, MJ has a basketball game at three-thirty."

"How do you know all this?" My head still felt fuzzy but none of this made any sense.

"MJ," she said. "He asked if I could take them today since

he couldn't reach you."

I hung my head. "I'm so sorry. I would never ask you to do that. Let me call MJ."

"I already told him yes. It's been a while since I've seen the kids."

Since when did she want to see the kids? She knew I still saw them regularly, and although she always asked how they were doing, she'd never suggested getting together with them. "But Maria will be there too. Are you sure you want to be there for that?"

"I'd like to meet her," Aunt Maddy said. "I need to run but we'll talk later."

She hung up before I could respond. I placed Jake's phone on the coffee table and closed my eyes. I could easily fall back asleep if I let myself. Then Jake's voice boomed, "What was that about?"

My eyes flashed open and for the first time since Jonah died I looked at Jake and didn't immediately think of Jonah. Now my first thought was *this man drugged me*. "I need to go," I said and stood up.

"You want some food first?" Jake asked as he followed me to the front door. "I can make you toast."

"You've done enough, thanks."

When I reached for the doorknob Jake stretched his arm out over my head, pinning the door shut. "Grace, I need that flash drive."

I turned around and stared up at him. "You've got to be kidding me."

"It's important. I wouldn't be asking if it wasn't."

"I couldn't give it to you even if I wanted to." And I definitely did not want to. "I don't have it on me."

"I know. It's in your safe deposit box. You told me last night," he answered my question before I could ask. "I can drive up next week and we can go to the bank together. You need to delete the file off your laptop too. Or better yet, trash the laptop. You didn't upload it to the cloud, did you?"

"I can't believe you think I would help you after what you did."

"You wouldn't just be helping me; you'd be helping yourself too. It's not safe for you to have that file."

I briefly entertained arguing the point with him, then opted for a simple, "Fuck you."

As soon as I arrived home I got in the shower and stayed there until my fingers pruned. But no matter how long I let the hot water wash over me, I still felt dirty. It wasn't just because I'd vomited and slept in my clothes. It was Jake who made me feel that way. I knew he hadn't taken advantage of me physically, but I still felt used.

After I showered, I took more acetaminophen and crawled into bed. But I turned the ringer up on my phone and left it on the nightstand so I would hear it if Aunt Maddy called.

It wasn't the phone that woke me.

Chapter 36

I woke to the incessant chime of my new doorbell, the one Daniel had installed for me before we'd broken up. It was synched to an app on my phone connected to the doorbell's camera. I tapped the phone and was surprised to see Brian Sullivan standing on my front porch.

I answered from the comfort of my bed. "Brian, what are you doing here?"

"Hi, Grace, can I come in?"

"This really isn't the best time," I said, pulling the covers up to my chin even though I knew Brian couldn't see me. The camera only worked one way. "Can I call you next week?"

"No, I really need to talk to you now."

I might have still said no if he didn't look so agitated. His eyes kept darting around and his face, which was always a bit flushed, seemed pinker and sweatier than usual. "Okay, give me a minute."

He gave the camera a tight smile. "Thanks, Grace."

I pulled on sweatpants and a clean T-shirt and hurried downstairs. "What's up, Brian?" I asked, locking the door behind him. "Can I get you something to drink?"

"No, no, I'm fine," he said, wiping the sweat off his forehead with the back of his hand. "Sorry to bother you again but it's important. Jonah had a home office, didn't he?"

"Yes, but he rarely worked from home." Which Brian should know since Jonah's office was next to his and he saw him there every weekday.

Brian glanced at the staircase, correctly assuming Jonah's office was upstairs. "May I take a look?"

"Why do you want to see Jonah's office?"

"I'd rather not say."

"Well, I'd rather you did say."

Brian stared at me a moment, probably trying to come up with some believable lie. Apparently, he couldn't think of one, so he said, "We're still looking for the flash drive."

"I told you, I already looked for it and it's not here."

"I know, but I promised the client I'd check myself."

"Which client?" I asked, half hoping and half dreading this client would have a Russian-sounding name.

"I really can't say. It's confidential. You're a lawyer. You understand."

"I wasn't aware California had an accountant-client privilege." I didn't know that for a fact, but I wasn't about to google it in front of Brian.

"This particular client requires confidentiality. Please, Grace, I'm asking you as a personal favor. I promise I won't take long."

I didn't trust Brian, or even like him, but I did feel sorry for him. I'd never seen him look so stressed. He wasn't a young man, and he was out of shape. Since I didn't want to be responsible for him having a heart attack in my hallway, I led him upstairs to our home office. I pointed to Jonah's desk, but Brian likely could've guessed since his was empty except for a blank computer screen and mine was stacked with manila file folders and yellow legal pads.

Brian sat down in Jonah's chair. "Would you mind if I look through it?"

I shrugged and he took that as assent. He probably would've preferred I left him alone, but I leaned against the doorframe and watched as he opened and closed each of Jonah's desk drawers. When that yielded nothing, he glanced around the room. "What's in the closet?" he asked.

"Boxes," I replied, and Brian's eyebrows raised. "They've been there since we moved in. I doubt you'll find anything useful in them but you're welcome to look."

Brian opened the accordion doors and pulled out three boxes Jonah and I had never bothered to unpack. The top one was filled with old tax returns and financial documents. I made a mental note to go through them after Brian left. Maybe some of those documents were old enough to be shredded. The second box was filled with books we didn't have room for on the bookshelves downstairs. I knew it was silly to keep saving them since I'd never read them again, but I loved paper books and could never throw them away. I'd go through them later and donate some to the library. The third box was filled with random junk—manuals for appliances we no longer owned, an old landline telephone, a coffee mug I thought had disappeared in the move. I grabbed the mug and set it on my desk.

Brian sifted through the contents of the third box until he triumphantly pulled out an old silver flash drive. I knew it was old because it was physically larger than the flash drives they sell now. Either Brian didn't notice, or he didn't care. He looked relieved and smiled for the first time since he'd arrived.

"Do you want to check it?" I asked. "You can use my computer."

"No, I've taken up enough of your time," he said, slipping

the flash drive into his pants pockets. "I'll make sure you get this back after IT downloads the files."

If Jonah was hiding something else, an old flash drive in a moving box I never would've thought to look in would've been a good place to stash it. But it was too late now. I wasn't going to wrestle Brian to get it back.

As we exited the office, Brian glanced at the closed door at the end of the hall. "What's in there?" he asked.

"My daughter's room."

Brian nodded and stared down, refusing to meet my eye.

THE NEXT MORNING I took Aunt Maddy out for brunch at her favorite beach café. I wanted to apologize to her for my behavior of late and I also wanted to hear what she thought of Maria. She only wanted to know why I spent the night at Jake's apartment. She thought my story was better than hers, and so did I.

"I still can't believe he drugged me," I said, dipping a bite of French toast into the pool of syrup on my plate.

"What choice did he have?" she replied, cutting off a chunk of omelet with her fork.

"What choice did he have?" I said, my voice rising. "How about not drugging me?"

Aunt Maddy glanced at the couple at the table next to ours, who were openly staring at us. We all smiled at each other and looked away.

"I can't believe you're defending him," I hissed.

"I'm not defending him," she said, her voice low too. "All I'm saying is you got him drunk and pumped him for information and he basically did the same thing to you."

"The part you seem to be missing here is the lack of consent. He drank voluntarily. I was drugged *involuntarily*. That's what makes it a crime."

She rolled her eyes. "What are you going to do? Have him arrested?"

"Of course not. I just have to assume he now knows everything I know and act accordingly."

"Meaning?"

"He wants me to give him the flash drive."

She swallowed a sip of her coffee. "And are you going to?"

"No. The flash drive is my leverage. It's the only way I'll ever find out the truth."

Chapter 37

THE MARINE LAYER burned off while we were eating breakfast, so by the time we left the restaurant it was sunny and warm outside. Aunt Maddy suggested we take advantage of the beautiful weather and go for a stroll along the beach. We hadn't walked far when we spotted the police vehicle on the sand and the crowd gathered behind it. We joined the spectators, thinking perhaps it was a shark attack. They were infrequent, but occasionally a surfer got bit.

It wasn't a shark attack. The gossip spreading through the crowd was that a local man had drowned after falling off his boat. A TV reporter doing a live spot told the camera the police had identified the man, but they weren't releasing his name because his family hadn't been notified yet. I said a silent prayer for his loved ones who didn't yet know that this beautiful Sunday morning was about to become the worst day of their lives.

I WAS GETTING ready for bed that night when Aunt Maddy called. "Are you watching the news?" she asked.

I spit my toothpaste into the sink and shut the faucet. "No, I was brushing my teeth. Why?"

"They're running the story on the man who drowned."

"So?" I asked, ripping off a piece of dental floss. "Are we on camera or something?"

"No, but the police released his name."

I didn't understand why she was so interested in this story. "Is it someone you know?" I asked, winding the dental floss around my index fingers.

"No, but I think it's someone you know."

"Who?"

"His name's Brian Sullivan."

By the time I'd switched on the television the anchors had moved on to the weather, but I was able to find the story on the TV station's website. They showed a photo so I knew it was Jonah's former boss and not just another local man who happened to have the same name.

According to the article, Brian's body had been discovered early this morning by local surfers. The Coast Guard had found his abandoned boat offshore. The police think alcohol may have played a part. The article noted he was survived by a wife, three children, and one grandchild. The family requested charitable donations be made in Brian's name in lieu of flowers.

I called Aunt Maddy back as soon as I finished reading. "Did they say anything on the news about suspecting foul play?"

"No. They just mentioned he wasn't wearing a life jacket."

"Don't you think that's odd?"

"That he wasn't wearing a life jacket? No, most people don't."

"No, that he accidentally fell off his boat and drowned."

Whatever happened to Brian Sullivan was no accident.

Chapter 38

THE LAST TIME I'd worn this dress was the day of Jonah and Amelia's funeral. Today I was wearing it to Brian Sullivan's wake. Aunt Maddy thought I should skip the wake and go directly to the police with my suspicions. I didn't think the police would believe me. It turned out we were both right.

The Sullivan's home was one of those stately old houses on the top of the bluff not far from where Daniel lived. The Sullivans didn't have an ocean view, but their home was situated on an oversized lot, which made it valuable.

It was a warm night so in addition to the mourners gathered on the first floor of the house, groups of people mingled on the front lawn too. It took me a while to find Kathy Sullivan standing under a giant oak tree. We'd only met once before at the firm's movie-themed holiday party. She and Brian had dressed up as Cleopatra and Marc Antony. I recognized her without her gold lamé dress and headband, but I didn't know if she would know me without the blonde wig and the hot pink suit.

"Of course, I remember you," Brian's wife, now widow, said when I introduced myself. She reached out and squeezed my hand and I instantly thought of my mother. Kathy was taller and had darker hair than my mom, but their scent was the same—Chanel No. 5. "We were all devastated by what happened to Jonah and your poor baby."

"Thank you," I replied. "I'm so sorry for your loss."

I could see the tears in her eyes in the light from the lanterns strung through the tree branches, but she forced a smile and thanked me.

"Could we speak for a moment in private?" I asked. The closest mourner was a few feet away, but this was not a conversation I wanted to take a chance someone would overhear.

The forced smile disappeared. "I don't think this is the right time, Grace."

"I wish it wasn't, but I'm afraid it is." The burial was scheduled for the next day. I lowered my voice and asked, "Can you tell me if Brian had an autopsy?"

Kathy took a step back. "I really don't think that's any of your concern."

A woman in her early twenties whose features were similar to Kathy's but whose age was much closer to mine appeared at Kathy's side. "Mom, are you okay?"

"Yes," she replied, but her eyes never left my face.

I turned to the younger woman. "I'm Grace Hughes. I knew your dad. I'm so sorry for your loss."

"Thank you," she replied. "How did you and my father know each other?"

The way she was looking at me had me wondering if she thought I was his mistress. Then I wondered if Kathy thought so too. It would explain why she was so hostile. "My husband used to work for your father. But that's not why I'm here. I have some information about your father's death I think you'll want to hear."

Rose Sullivan led me into the house and her mother reluctantly followed. She flicked on the lights in a room, which I guessed from the diplomas hanging on the wall behind the large wooden desk had been her father's office. Rose sat in Brian's desk chair, and I perched on the edge of the brown leather sofa. Rose suggested her mother sit down too, but Kathy said she preferred to stand. She stood next to the window looking out onto the front yard.

"What is this about?" Rose asked.

I wasn't sure where to start. I felt compelled to share my suspicions, but I hadn't planned out the conversation in my head. "Your father came to see me last Saturday. He just showed up at my house."

"Do you know why?" Rose asked.

"He was looking for a flash drive he thought belonged to my husband."

"Then he came to see your husband?" Rose asked, seemingly confused.

"Her husband's dead," Kathy said, still staring out the window. "And now mine is too."

Rose's eyes widened. Kathy's accusatory tone seemed to surprise Rose as much as it did me. Did Kathy think I was somehow responsible for Brian's death? I chalked it up to grief.

"My husband died almost two years ago. My daughter too."

"I'm so sorry," Rose said.

I swallowed hard. I didn't want to get sidetracked. "But the reason I'm here, the reason I wanted to speak with your mom, is about that flash drive."

Rose looked at me expectantly. "I don't understand. What does a flash drive have to do with anything?"

I explained to Rose that I had contacted the firm a few weeks ago. "That's when your father told me they'd found some irregularities in my husband's work—"

"What kind of irregularities?" Rose asked.

"I don't know. Your father wouldn't tell me. But when I told him I found a flash drive I thought had belonged to my husband, your father wanted it. He was quite insistent that I give it to him."

"And did you?" she asked.

I hadn't planned on lying to her, but with Kathy glaring at me as if I was the one who'd murdered Brian, I didn't want to admit the truth. "I gave him *a* flash drive but, apparently, it wasn't the right one because your father called me a few days later and asked me to look again. I told him the one I gave him was the only one I found, and it was after that conversation that your father showed up at my house. He wanted to come inside and look for the flash drive himself. He seemed very agitated."

"Agitated?"

"Stressed. Very stressed. So I let him search."

"And did he find what he was looking for?"

"I don't know. He looked through some boxes my husband had stored in the closet and there was a flash drive in there, but I don't know what was on it. I offered to let him use my computer to check, but he just took the flash drive with him and left."

Rose turned to Kathy. "Mom, did you know anything about this?"

"No," she replied. "Your father's business was your father's business. I didn't interfere."

Rose turned back to me. "I don't understand. Why are you telling us this?"

"Because I don't think your father's death was an accident."

Her forehead wrinkled and her eyes widened. "What do you think happened to him? You think someone pushed him overboard to get a flash drive?" Rose's tone told me how ludicrous she thought my suggestion was.

"For what was on the flash drive. Or, more likely, what wasn't on the flash drive."

Rose glanced over at Kathy. "Mom, are you listening to this?"

Kathy turned away from the window and folded her arms across her chest. "I think you need to leave."

I stood up and directed my words at Kathy. "The reason I'm here is because I think whoever killed Jonah killed Brian too. If we went to the police together—"

"The man who murdered your husband is dead," Kathy said. "I don't know why—"

"Wait," Rose said and stood up too. "Your husband was *murdered*?"

"Yes." She'd probably assumed they died in a car accident. Most people did.

"But the man who did it is dead," Kathy said. "So he couldn't have killed Brian."

"The man who pulled the trigger is dead," I said. "But whoever ordered him to do it is still alive."

Rose shifted her gaze from me to Kathy. Her voice cracked when she spoke. "Mom, was Daddy involved in something he shouldn't have been?"

Kathy crossed the room and held her daughter's face in her hands. "Of course not, darling. Your father was a good man."

Then Kathy wiped away Rose's tears with her thumbs and turned back to me. "I don't know if you're having some sort of mental breakdown or you're just delusional, but I want no part of it. Brian fell off his boat and drowned. You need to leave this house now and never contact us again."

I stared into Kathy's steely blue eyes. *She knows.*

Chapter 39

I hurried down the block to where I'd parked the car. As soon as I was inside, I called Aunt Maddy. I knew I sounded hysterical, and I didn't care.

"You need to calm down," Aunt Maddy said.

"But she knows," I cried. "She knows and she doesn't care."

"Just breathe," she said. "Are you okay to drive?"

"Yes." *Breathe in for four, hold for four, breathe out for six.*

"Then come straight to my house. I'm closer and we'll figure out what to do next."

Aunt Maddy must've been watching for my car because as soon as I pulled into her driveway, she opened the front door.

"Don't be mad," she said when I reached her porch. "But I called Dr. Rubenstein."

"Why would you call Dr. Rubenstein? I told you I was taking a break from therapy."

"Because I'm worried about you. I knew going to Brian's wake was a mistake."

"It wasn't a mistake," I said, following Aunt Maddy into the house. The deep breathing exercises had helped. It was the only useful thing I took away from my time at the Wellstone Center. "Now I know his wife knows. She isn't in the dark like I was."

"Or maybe she is in the dark and she just wants to stay there."

I spent the night at Aunt Maddy's house. I knew I'd be fine if I went home, but my aunt didn't, so to put her mind at ease, I stayed. But I tossed and turned all night. When I woke up with the sun, I knew I'd never fall back asleep, so I got up and dressed. Aunt Maddy must've heard me stirring because she knocked on my bedroom door.

"You okay?" she asked.

I zipped up my funeral dress and opened my door. "I'm going home to shower and change before I head to the office."

"Do you have a lot of work to do?"

"Not really." Janelle was no longer referring cases to me, and I hadn't made any effort to obtain new clients on my own. "But today is Janelle's last day, so I thought I should be there to say goodbye."

"It might be better if you weren't. Besides, it's a beautiful morning. Wouldn't you rather go for a walk on the beach with your favorite aunt?"

"In this?" I asked, looking down at my dress and matching black heels.

"You can borrow something of mine."

My aunt obviously didn't trust me to be alone. "I'm not going to try to kill myself again if that's what you're worried about. You know that, right?"

"I love you," Aunt Maddy said. "Please come walk with me."

We picked up coffees at Starbucks and brought them with us to the beach. The sky was cloudless, but it was still cool outside so I zipped up my borrowed sweatshirt and donned the baseball cap Aunt Maddy insisted I wear after I refused her offer to douse my face in sunscreen.

The beach was empty except for a handful of early morning walkers and a small group of people, mostly women, doing yoga on the sand. I pushed my sunglasses down my nose to get a better look.

"Oh my god, that's Felicity." I recognized her even with her mane of jet black hair pulled into a messy bun on top of her head. Her hot pink yoga outfit was hard to miss.

"Who?" Aunt Maddy asked.

"Felicity. The patient advocate from the Wellstone Center. You met her at the hearing for my release."

"Oh, right." Aunt Maddy said. We watched as the yogis effortlessly moved from warrior pose to lotus. After a few minutes of sitting cross legged on their mats, there was a chorus of Namaste and they all stood up. "Did you want to say hello?" my aunt asked. "It looks like they're done."

I hadn't planned on talking to Felicity, but there was no reason not to. I'd always liked her. We stepped off the cement path that ran parallel to the ocean and onto the sand. Felicity was talking with another woman when she spotted us approaching.

"Grace?" she called out.

I smiled and waved. "I see you finally made it to sunrise yoga."

Felicity said goodbye to her friend and jogged over to me and Aunt Maddy. "It's so good to see you. Can I give you a hug?"

"Sure," I replied, and she practically flung herself at me.

"I'm so happy you're doing better. You look terrific."

"Thanks," I said. "You look good too."

She glanced down at her Lycra-clad thighs and frowned. "I've lost fifteen pounds, but I've still got another ten to go."

Aunt Maddy shook her head. "You girls need to stop obsessing over your weight. You look fine as you are."

Felicity smiled at her. "You're Grace's aunt, right?"

"Yes," Aunt Maddy and I both answered.

"What are you doing here?" Felicity asked. "Just out for a walk on the beach?"

"Yes, I'm still an early riser," I said. "Unfortunately. How often do you come to sunrise yoga?"

"Every day since I got laid off," Felicity said, then reached into her bag for her sweatshirt and pulled it over her head.

"Oh my god," I said. "I'm so sorry. When did it happen?"

"Last month."

"I'm sure you'll find another job soon," Aunt Maddy said.

Felicity shook her head. "I've started my own business. I'm influencer now. You should check out my videos. I already have over ten thousand followers."

I had no idea whether ten thousand followers was a good amount, but Felicity obviously thought it was. "Definitely," I said.

"What have you been up to?" she asked. "Did you ever talk to Dr. Rubenstein?"

"Yes," I said. Then Aunt Maddy added, "As a matter of fact, Grace has an appointment with her this afternoon."

I shot Aunt Maddy an angry look but didn't contradict her. It was true she had made an appointment for me with Dr. Rubenstein for this afternoon. I just hadn't decided yet whether to keep it.

"My mom just loves her," Felicity said. "She really helped after my brother died."

"I'm so sorry," I said. "I didn't know you lost your brother."

"We're not supposed to share personal information with clients," Felicity replied. "One of the many rules I no longer have to follow. My brother died of an overdose. My mom was devastated. She felt like it was her fault, that she'd failed him somehow. Dr. Rubenstein really helped her. You seem like she's helped you too."

"She did." Regardless of how I felt about Dr. Rubenstein at the moment, I had to admit I was a lot better now than I was when we'd first met, and I had to give her credit for that.

Felicity pulled out her phone and thumbed the screen until she found my contact information. "I'm texting you a link to my videos. If you like them, please share with your friends." We hugged goodbye, then Aunt Maddy and I resumed our walk along the beach path.

For a few minutes the only sounds we heard were the seagulls' calls and the waves crashing on the wet sand. I knew Aunt Maddy held back for as long as she could but, eventually, she cracked. "It sounds like Dr. Rubenstein really knows what she's doing."

I stared at her over the top of my sunglasses. "Really?"

"Please, Grace. If you won't do it for yourself, then do it for me."

Apparently, the willingness to emotionally blackmail one's family is an inherited trait.

Aunt Maddy insisted on driving me to my appointment with Dr. Rubenstein. I didn't think it was worth arguing about, so I agreed. I figured she'd just read a magazine in the waiting room during my session. Aunt Maddy had other ideas.

Chapter 40

Dr. Rubenstein and I both stared after my aunt as she walked down the hall ahead of us and entered my therapist's office.

"Are we having a joint session today?" Dr. Rubenstein asked me.

I shrugged. "If we are, it's news to me."

We both followed Aunt Maddy inside. I took a seat on the couch, but not in my usual spot since Aunt Maddy was already sitting there. Dr. Rubenstein stood by the open door. "I'm sorry, Madeline, but this is Grace's session. I must ask you to leave. But I'd be happy to make an appointment for you if you'd like to see me as well."

"I think I should stay," Aunt Maddy said.

"Why is that?" Dr. Rubenstein asked.

"I'm the one who convinced Grace to come today. I'd like to see for myself what goes on here."

Dr. Rubenstein turned to me. "This is your decision, Grace."

"Do you ever do joint sessions?" She and I had only ever met one-on-one.

"Yes, for marriage counseling and family therapy. And I will allow another person to join an individual session, if a client requests it and I think it would be helpful. But it's something we normally discuss in advance. While this is highly unusual, I'm not opposed to letting your aunt stay if that's what you want."

I didn't see any downside in letting her stay, especially since I'd only agreed to come to shut her up. "It's fine," I said. "It'll save me the trouble of telling her what happened on the drive home."

Dr. Rubenstein cracked a smile. "As you wish," she said and shut the door behind her.

It felt weird being back. Not just because Aunt Maddy was there too, but because she was sitting in my usual spot. I'd never sat on the other end of the couch before. It gave me an entirely different view of the room.

Dr. Rubenstein spoke first. "I'm glad you decided to come back."

"I didn't," I said. "Aunt Maddy made the appointment."

"Yes, but you decided to keep it and you didn't have to."

"You can thank Felicity for that," I said.

Dr. Rubenstein cocked her head to the side like a dog. "Felicity?"

"She was my patient advocate at the Wellstone Center. She's the one who referred me to you."

Dr. Rubenstein nodded. "Oh yes, Felicity Tran. I didn't realize you kept in touch with her."

"I don't. We ran into her at the beach this morning. Did you know she got laid off and now she's an influencer?"

"No, I didn't know that."

"She mentioned her brother died of an overdose and that you really helped her mom. I guess that's why I came back."

Dr. Rubenstein nodded but remained silent.

After maybe thirty seconds, Aunt Maddy said, "Aren't the two of you going to talk?"

Dr. Rubenstein smiled patiently. "Grace will speak when she's ready."

Aunt Maddy turned to me. "What are you waiting for?" She tapped her watch. "Time's a ticking."

"You're the one who wanted to come today. Why don't you talk."

So she did. She started to tell Dr. Rubenstein about my evening with Jake but she got the details wrong, so I jumped in and finished the story, then told Dr. Rubenstein about my visit from Brian Sullivan, his drowning, and my conversation with his family at the wake.

"That's a lot," Dr. Rubenstein said.

"It is," I agreed.

Then we sat in silence again as Aunt Maddy glanced back and forth between me and Dr. Rubenstein. "How long are you two going to just sit there and stare at each other? Isn't this session only an hour?"

"Fifty minutes," Dr. Rubenstein replied. "Maybe you should talk, Madeline. You seem to have something you want to say."

"I think you should tell Grace she needs to go to the police."

Dr. Rubenstein turned to me. "Is that what you want to do?"

"No, because they're not going to believe me. They're going to think I'm delusional, just like Brian's widow. And you."

"I don't think you're delusional," Dr. Rubenstein said. "In our last session I merely pointed out that there were alternative explanations for the things you were upset about."

"And now?" I asked.

"There are still alternative explanations," Dr. Rubenstein said, "but I agree the coincidences are piling up. I think at this point we're all too close to the situation to be objective. I think it would be helpful to get a third party's opinion."

"Another therapist?" I asked.

"No," Dr. Rubenstein said. "I was thinking more along the lines of law enforcement."

"I just told you I'm not going to the police."

"I know," Dr. Rubenstein said. "I have someone else in mind."

I MET Agent Gonzalez the next morning at a diner in the Bluffs. She'd chosen the restaurant because it was close to Dr. Rubenstein's house. Deena Gonzalez was both a DEA agent and Dr. Rubenstein's daughter-in-law. She and Dr. Rubenstein's daughter lived in San Diego, but they drove up to Santa Veneta for the weekend to celebrate Dr. Rubenstein's husband's sixtieth birthday. Dr. Rubenstein's son lived in Portugal and wasn't able to fly home for the celebration. I'd learned more about my therapist's personal life in six minutes with Deena Gonzalez than I had in six months of twice weekly sessions with her.

I knew Agent Gonzalez was the woman I was looking for even before she came up to me and introduced herself. There was no DEA insignia on her jeans or fitted T-shirt, but with her hair pulled back in a tight ponytail and her face make-up free, she gave off the same no-nonsense, law-enforcement vibe as Jake. She also happened to be the only other woman standing alone outside the restaurant. Everyone else milling about was part of a couple or a family.

We were seated at a booth next to the front window. We both ordered coffee and perused the menu. After the waitress took our food order—avocado toast for Deena and a bagel with cream cheese for me—I thanked her for agreeing to meet with me.

"Helen can be very persuasive," Deena replied, straightening her silverware.

My silverware was crooked too, but I didn't care. "How much did she tell you?"

When Deena's fork, knife, and spoon were perfectly parallel, she clasped her hands together and leaned in. "Very little. She said you needed an objective opinion. I really have no idea why I'm here today. Are you involved in a drug case?"

I sat back and considered the question. "I don't think so. Although I suppose I could be. I really have no idea."

Deena laughed and I noticed she had a beautiful smile. Her lips were a deep pink, even without lipstick, and her teeth, like her utensils, were perfectly straight. "People involved in a drug case usually know. Why don't you just tell me what happened."

Deena didn't take notes and only occasionally interrupted to ask a question. By the time I finished talking, she'd cleaned her plate and my bagel was cold.

Deena waited for the waitress to refill her coffee and leave again before she spoke. "I'm not really sure what you and Helen want from me. This is out of my jurisdiction."

"I don't think either one of us expected you to do anything. We just wanted an objective third party to tell us whether there's something to this or if I'm just crazy."

Deena smiled. "I'll leave it to my mother-in-law to make the determination about your mental state. That's her area of expertise, not mine, although you seem sane enough to me. If you're asking me if I think a crime has been committed, the answer is I don't know. But there's enough here to open an investigation."

I blew out the breath I didn't realize I'd been holding. "And who would do the investigation?"

She tapped her polish-free fingernail on the table. "That's where it gets sticky. I assume it was the local police who investigated your husband's killing and presumably the same local police who concluded Brian Sullivan's death was an accident."

"Yes. Do you think if I went back to them and told them what I know and gave them the flash drive they would investigate?"

"Unlikely. But you could take this to the FBI."

"Anyone in particular at the FBI? I can't ask my brother-in-law for a referral for obvious reasons."

"What's his name again?"

"Jacob Hughes. He worked at the LA office, but he left a few years ago."

"Let me make some calls and get back to you. I would think at a minimum the FBI would want to take a look at the flash drive."

I DROVE straight from the diner to Tim and Richard's house to pick up MJ and Sofia for their supervised visit with Maria. My aunt filled in for me last week, but today would be my first time. Usually, Tim was the one home with the baby and Richard drove the older kids around, but today it was the reverse.

"Where is everyone?" I asked Richard, then smiled at baby Aaron, who was strapped to his chest. I'd replaced the baby carrier that Alex had destroyed.

"MJ and Sofia are upstairs, but I was hoping we could talk for a minute first. Tim's out with Isaiah and Ethan."

"Sure," I said, reaching out to squeeze Aaron's chubby feet. He gurgled in response. Then I followed Richard into the kitchen.

"Can I get you anything?" he asked, pouring himself a glass of water.

"No thanks," I said, sitting down on a stool at the island. "What's up?"

"Makeyla moved out last week."

I nodded. "My aunt told me. How's Sofia doing? I heard she was upset."

"She made a new friend in dance class, so that's helped."

"Great." I waited for Richard to continue, but he just rubbed his finger along a scratch etched into the countertop. "Was that it?" I asked surreptitiously glancing at my watch. I didn't want to be late.

He laid his hand flat on the counter and looked up. "No. Tim and I have been doing a lot of talking lately...about our family...about what we can realistically handle. The thing is, now that we have Aaron, we can't really foster as many children anymore."

"Oh," I said because I didn't know what else to say.

"In some ways the older kids are easier," Richard continued. "They're more self-sufficient. But they come with other challenges and, frankly, neither one of us is up to it right now."

I nodded.

"But we care about these kids. We don't want to just abandon them."

"Of course." I was certainly in no position to judge.

"Tim and I talked to the social worker yesterday, and she's going to start looking for alternative placements. We haven't told the kids yet though, so please don't say anything to MJ or Sofia."

"I won't. I promise." My mind was racing. What would happen to Sofia and MJ now? Maria had petitioned to regain custody, but she hadn't even found a job yet. There was no way the court would grant her custody of the kids at this point. They would have to go to another foster home.

"We wanted to tell you though. Confidentially. Because of how close you are with MJ. Tim thought—"

We heard feet thundering down the stairs and seconds later

MJ appeared in the kitchen. "Hey, Grace. I didn't know you were here. Are we leaving?"

"Yes," I said, reaching for my purse and praying he hadn't heard any of our conversation. "Whenever you and Sofia are ready."

"Cool, cool," MJ said. "Can we stop for food on the way?"

"Didn't you just eat breakfast a couple hours ago?" Richard asked.

MJ pulled opened the refrigerator and stared inside. "Yeah, so?"

I laughed as Richard shook his head. "I don't think we have time to stop for food before your visit, but we can go to lunch afterwards if you want."

"Okay," MJ said and shut the fridge door. Then he shouted upstairs for Sofia, who appeared at the bottom of the staircase in a light pink leotard and matching tights. "Get your shoes on. Grace is taking us to see Mama."

Sofia waved at me and ran back up the steps.

I turned to Richard, who gave me a meaningful look. He hadn't come out and asked me to foster MJ and Sofia again, but I was sure that was his intention. MJ must not have told him or Tim about my suicide attempt either. The kid sure knew how to keep a secret.

Chapter 41

MARIA WAS WAITING for us on a picnic bench at the entrance to the park. She looked better today than she had the last time I'd seen her at the Wellstone Center. She'd gained a little weight and her skin was less sallow.

As soon as Sofia saw her mother, she sprinted to her and hugged her around the waist. MJ approached Maria too, but more slowly and he only gave her a quick peck on the cheek. I joined them but kept a few feet of distance between us. I didn't know if Maria remembered me, so I reintroduced myself. "We met at the Wellstone Center."

"Yes." Her reply wasn't unfriendly, but it didn't invite conversation either.

I pointed to a bench across from the swings. "I'll be over there if you need me."

She nodded and returned her attention to her kids.

I tried not to make it too obvious I was watching them. I kept my phone in my hand and occasionally glanced down at it as I studied their interactions. When it came to Sofia, Maria acted like any other doting mother. She pushed her daughter on the swing and followed her around as she played on the climbing structure. Her interactions with MJ were more stilted, but I blamed him. MJ spent most of the visit standing next to her with his arms folded across his chest and a sour expression on his face. I thought about saying something to him but didn't think I should interfere. I was supposed to be supervising this visit, not orchestrating it.

When the hour was up, I joined them and told them it was time to go. Sofia clung to her mother, but MJ seemed relieved. Maria whispered something to Sofia in Spanish, but whatever she told her didn't calm her. Sofia cried all the way back to the car.

"It's okay, Sofia," MJ said. "We'll see Mama again next week."

That didn't stop her tears either. I felt so helpless I offered the only thing I could think of to make her happy. "Who wants ice cream?"

That cheered her up.

TIM AND RICHARD and baby Aaron were sitting on a blanket on the front lawn when I pulled up with MJ and Sofia. Instead of just dropping them off, which had been my intention, I parked and walked them to the house.

"Who's taking me to dance class?" Sofia asked.

Richard glanced at his watch. "I will. Go get your stuff."

Sofia ran into the house and MJ followed her. But when Sofia reappeared a minute later with a pink ballerina bag slung over her shoulder, MJ wasn't with her. Richard and Sofia left, and I sat down on the blanket with Tim and the baby.

"Richard told me he told you," Tim said, his voice low. Maybe he was concerned MJ was lurking somewhere he could overhear us.

"Yes," I replied as I dangled the colorful plastic keys above

Aaron's head. He stared at them but was still too young to reach for them.

"What do you think?" he asked.

I tried to be diplomatic. "You need to do what you think is best. If that means no more fostering then—"

"Not about that." He lowered his voice to a whisper. "Do you think you'd want to foster MJ and Sofia again?"

I sighed. I wasn't prepared for this conversation. "I don't know. I need to talk to my aunt."

"We just thought since you obviously still care about them..."

"I know," I whispered, "but it's not that simple."

"To be honest, we never really understood why you gave them up in the first place."

When I didn't respond, Tim continued. "I asked MJ once, but he wouldn't say. Richard thought maybe there'd been some sort of incident."

I could only imagine what he was thinking. "No, nothing like that." I took a deep breath and continued. "To make a long story short, it was my aunt who wanted to give them up. Not because she didn't bond with them, but the opposite. She became very attached to Sofia, and when their mother resurfaced and wanted to regain custody, my aunt couldn't deal with it. She thought if she had to give them up it was better to cut ties sooner rather than later."

"That's always a possibility when you foster," Tim said. "But you know that going in."

"Yes, but this was our first time fostering and we weren't emotionally prepared. My aunt only agreed to take them in on an emergency basis because I asked her to. The whole thing was my idea."

"And they won't let you foster alone because you're a single parent? That seems very shortsighted."

I shook my head. I really didn't want to have to tell him about my suicide attempt. "It's more than just that."

"I understand it's harder as a single parent," he continued. "I could never do this alone. But, Grace, unlike most of us, you can afford to hire help."

Tim waited for me to explain. When I didn't, he said, "You don't have to tell me if you're not comfortable sharing."

I laughed. "Except you really want me to."

Tim laughed too. "Of course, I want you to! Richard and I have been trying to figure this out since the day we met you."

"And what have you come up with? Surely you must have a theory."

"Well, like I said, at first we thought something bad must've happened, but MJ denied it. And as we got to you know better, we really couldn't picture it. Now Richard thinks you don't want the responsibility, that you want your freedom."

"Is that what you think too?" I asked.

"No. I think that's what Richard wants."

We both laughed.

Tim hesitated then said, "I think the real reason is you only want MJ, not Sofia too."

I stared down at the blanket.

"That's nothing to be ashamed of," Tim continued. "Not everyone is as crazy as I am and wants a bunch of kids. My husband, for example. He thinks one is plenty."

"That's not it," I said. "I should've tried harder with Sofia though. It's just that when I'm with her, I can't help thinking of Amelia. And my aunt was so good with her, I gave myself permission to step back. That's still no excuse."

Tim reached for my hand. "No one blames you, Grace. It's completely understandable."

"To you, maybe."

"To everyone," Tim said. "And MJ didn't want to be separated from Sofia?"

I shook my head. "But it wouldn't have mattered anyway because that's not why they don't live with me." I stared at his expectant face. "They wouldn't approve me. That's why it had to be my aunt."

"CPS wouldn't approve you?" Tim roared, startling baby Aaron, who began to cry. Tim picked him up and rubbed circles on his back until he quieted down again. "That's ridiculous," Tim said, his voice low again. "Did Serena tell you that? Because I'll call her right now and tell her she's crazy."

He pulled his phone out of his back pocket and looked like he was actually going to call, so I said, "Don't. She had nothing to do with it." I realized then there was no way out of this, so I took a deep breath and told him the whole story.

Tim was still indignant. "You made a mistake. We all screw up sometimes. Are they going to hold it against you forever?"

"Not forever. But Janelle told me I'd need to wait at least a year."

"I think you should apply now. Serena's already looking for a new placement. You know, Grace, not all foster parents get into this for the right reasons. Some of the homes—"

"I know. I'm going to talk to my aunt. I promise."

I DECIDED the best time to broach the topic with Aunt Maddy would be over an alcohol-infused Sunday brunch. She was on her second mimosa when my phone rang. I was surprised to see Deena Gonzalez's name in the caller ID.

"Is this a good time?" Deena asked when I picked up.

The restaurant was loud, and she must've heard the noise. "Actually, can I call you back?"

"I just need to know if you're available to meet with

someone from the FBI's LA field office next week. The meeting shouldn't take more than a couple hours."

"Sure. Is this a friend of yours?"

"No, I don't know him, but he works with your brother-in-law. He's Jacob's boss."

I was sure I'd misheard Deena and asked her to repeat what she'd said. But I hadn't misheard. The person Deena wanted me to meet at the FBI's LA field office was Jake's boss.

"You mean *former* boss. I told you, Jake left the FBI a few years ago. He works for a private security company now."

"I think you're misinformed," Deena said. "Your brother-in-law has been an agent in the LA field office for the past seven years."

Chapter 42

I ENDED the call with Deena and stared across the table at my aunt.

"What's wrong?" she asked, her fork frozen in the air above her plate. "Who were you talking to?"

"Dr. Rubenstein's daughter-in-law. The DEA agent. And you're not going to believe what she just told me." I repeated the short conversation to my aunt. "Jake's been lying to us for years."

"Don't jump to conclusions," Aunt Maddy said. "You don't know that."

"I do know that. She just told me."

"Then I'm sure there's a reasonable explanation. Jake wouldn't lie to us for no reason."

"The reason is he's a fucking liar. And who knows what else he's been lying about. Maybe he's the one who killed Jonah and Amelia and he just lied about the other guy to protect himself."

The people seated at the tables on either side of us were now openly staring at us. I didn't care, but Aunt Maddy did. "Stop it, Grace," she hissed. "You know that's not true."

"Do I?" I said, lowering my voice. "I don't think I know anything anymore."

197

We'd both lost our appetite, so I paid the bill and we left. I'd driven us to the restaurant so my aunt could drink, but she insisted on driving home and I didn't object. It meant I could focus all my fury on Jake.

She hadn't even pulled out of the parking lot yet when I called him. "You fucking liar!" I screamed when he picked up on the third ring.

"Let me explain," he said quietly.

I could hear voices in the background, so I knew he wasn't alone. "Explain what?" I yelled, hoping whoever he was with could hear me too. "Why you lied to us for *years*?"

"It wasn't like that."

"In what way was it not like that, Jake? I remember when you told us you were leaving the FBI. You said you were tired of putting your life on the line every day for no money. That you could double your salary in the private sector."

"All true," Jake said. "Except I never left."

"That's kind of a big exception, don't you think?"

"I can't have this conversation now," he said, lowering his voice even more. "Where are you?"

"I'm with my aunt."

"Wait for me at your aunt's house. I can be there in two hours and I'll explain everything."

HE MUST'VE SPED the entire way up the coast because it only took him an hour and a half. Or maybe he'd started from somewhere closer than LA. Wherever he left from, he definitely hadn't showered first. His T-shirt and basketball shorts were damp with sweat and he smelled awful. Aunt Maddy got one whiff of him and suggested we talk outside. We all filed out to the back patio, but only she and Jake sat down. I paced back and forth in front of them.

"Why, Jake? Bad enough lying to me, but Jonah was your brother, your best friend. How could you lie to him?"

Jake, who was sitting on the foot of the lounge chair with his head hanging down, looked up at me. "I never lied to Jonah."

"Liar! I was there, Jake. I heard it myself."

Jake shook his head. "That conversation was for your benefit. Jonah made me do it."

I stopped pacing. "Jonah asked you to lie to me?"

"Yes."

But Jake was a proven liar, so there was no reason to think he was telling the truth now. "And why would he do that?"

"The same reason I agreed. To protect you."

I threw my arms up. *We're back to this again?* "Protect me from what, Jake?"

He sighed and hung his head down.

"Jake," Aunt Maddy said gently, "I understand you thought you were protecting Grace. But it's gone too far now. People have died. You have to tell the truth. It's time."

Jake ran his hands through his hair and blew out his breath. "Do you think I could have something to drink?"

"Sure," Aunt Maddy said and stood up. "What can I get you? Water? Iced tea? I could make a pitcher of lemonade if you'd like."

Jake shot her his best smile. "I was thinking of something a little stronger."

Aunt Maddy smiled back. She always did have a soft spot for Jake. "Wine or spirits? I'm out of beer."

"Spirits," he said. "Whatever you've got is fine."

Jake and I didn't speak while we waited for Aunt Maddy to return. He remained seated on the foot of his lounge chair and scrolled through messages on his phone while I silently fumed. When Aunt Maddy reappeared with a bottle of bourbon, a bucket of ice, and three glasses, Jake poured himself two fingers and downed it like a shot. Then he poured himself a second one. Aunt Maddy filled her own glass with ice and added a splash of bourbon. I left my glass untouched. I didn't want to consume anything that might impair my abilities.

"You have to believe me," Jake said.

"No," I replied. "I don't. You've severely impeached your own credibility, Jacob."

Jake rolled his eyes. "Don't lawyer me."

"Then stop lying to me," I shot back.

"I'm not lying! We were trying to protect you."

Now I rolled my eyes. "Yes, your all-purpose excuse. Anytime you don't want to answer my question, you just tell me it's for my own protection. I know you think that somehow gets you off the hook, but it doesn't."

"She's right, Jake," Aunt Maddy said, upholding and over-ruling objections like a judge. "Why don't you start by telling us why you deceived us about leaving the FBI."

Jake nodded at Aunt Maddy then turned his attention back to me. "It was Jonah's idea."

I snorted. "Blame the dead guy. Good strategy, Jake."

He jumped up from the chair with his fists at his side. "It's the truth! I actually wanted Jonah to tell you because I thought you'd talk him out of it."

"Out of what?" Aunt Maddy asked.

"Out of helping me." Jake said and sat back down. He dropped his head in his hands and it felt like minutes passed before he looked up again. "Don't you see? I'm responsible. They died because of me."

Chapter 43

"WHAT DO you mean they died because of you?" Aunt Maddy looked stricken at his confession, but I remained stony.

Jake downed his second bourbon and ran his fingers through his hair again. He looked distraught. If he was lying to me now, then it was an Oscar-worthy performance.

"He took a meeting for me." Jake held up his index finger. "One meeting."

"What kind of meeting?" I asked. "Who did he meet with?"

"The Russians," he said. "Like your buddy Alex told you."

"How did—"

"The night you were at my house," Jake said.

"You mean the night you drugged me."

"After you got me drunk and searched my things."

I wanted to argue he drank that alcohol voluntarily whereas he had drugged me without my consent, but I wanted answers to my questions more than I wanted to be proven right. "Why would you ask Jonah to go to a meeting with Russian mobsters?"

"I didn't," Jake said. "I was totally against the idea. He insisted." Jake poured himself more bourbon, but this time he only took a sip instead of swigging the entire glass. "He'd been helping me with my cover. I was posing as an accountant so I could infiltrate their organization."

"An accountant?" I scoffed.

"You've heard the saying *follow the money*? Well, that's what I was doing. I was trying to infiltrate their money-laundering operation."

I had a sudden flash of memory of Jonah and Jake talking about the best ways to move money through shell corporations without leaving a paper trail. The only thing that stood out to me about the conversation was that they'd stopped talking when I'd walked into the room, which was odd. It's not as if I didn't know what my husband did for a living. I'd jokingly reminded Jonah that I couldn't testify against him because I was his wife. He'd laughed and changed the subject.

"So you were working undercover as an accountant for the Russian mob and you decided it would be a good idea to have Jonah, a private citizen with no law enforcement training, fill in for you? What? Did you have a dentist appointment that day you couldn't reschedule?"

Jake shot me an angry look. "It wasn't like that. The head of the organization had a nephew, some hot shot who'd made a few bucks dabbling in crypto and thought that made him a financial genius. The nephew thought he, not me, should be running the financial side of the business. His uncle didn't think he was ready yet, but the nephew was making things difficult for me, asking a lot of questions, things Jonah would know the answer to off the top of his head, but I didn't. My boss was getting concerned and considered pulling me out."

"So, you decided to risk my husband's life instead?"

"No, Jonah decided. I told him I thought it was a bad idea. If things went south in the meeting, he wouldn't know what to do. But he was convinced he could handle it. He said he met with clients all the time and knew how to close the deal. And I'd invested a year and a half of my life into this investigation. I didn't want to just walk away. That's a decision I'll have to live with for the rest of my life."

We waited for Jake to continue. When he didn't, Aunt Maddy prodded him. "Something went wrong at the meeting?"

"No, it was a huge success. Jonah did exactly what he said he'd do. He gave them a big presentation like he did for his legitimate clients. Told them he could get their tax rate down to zero, and it was all one hundred percent legal."

That I believed. I'd heard Jonah give that same speech over the phone when he'd taken work calls during his paternity leave.

"The head of the organization was so impressed," Jake continued, "he turned everything over to Jonah, or me, thinking I was Jonah, who was supposed to be me."

"Then what happened?" Aunt Maddy asked.

"Brian Sullivan happened," Jake said.

Chapter 44

"I KNEW IT!" I pounded my fist in my hand. "I knew Brian Sullivan was up to his neck in this."

Jake gave me an odd look. "Brian Sullivan wasn't part of this."

"But you just said—"

Jake shook his head. "You misunderstood. I had Jonah set up the accounts, but I told him not to keep any information at the office or use the firm's network. This needed to be completely walled off from the firm's legitimate accounts. But Brian found out and thought Jonah was setting up a side gig to steal clients. Jonah was afraid he was going to get fired so he made up some bullshit story about how this particular client was very secretive and required all kinds of extra security, blah, blah, blah."

"And Brian believed that?" I asked.

"I don't know what he believed. All he cared about was that the firm got its two and twenty management fee, which was a problem since I'd sold the Russians on a flat fifteen percent. One thing you should know about these guys is they're ridiculously cheap. They're always looking for a deal and pride themselves on never paying retail for anything. And if they can steal it instead of paying for it, that's always their preference, no matter how much money they have."

"And Brian wouldn't agree to fifteen?" I asked.

"Jonah didn't want to go there. He thought he'd ask too many questions. Plus he'd seen some, shall we say, questionable business practices involving some of Brian's legitimate clients."

"What does that mean?" Aunt Maddy asked.

"Well, I'm not saying the guy's Bernie Madoff, but if you've got money invested with him, I suggest you move it. Brian's been known to inflate earnings statements to make his results look better than they are, then use borrowed money to make up the difference. When Jonah told me what he found, I tipped off the SEC and they opened their own investigation. But that investigation ran parallel to ours; there was no crossover. The SEC just knew not to look into any of the accounts Jonah set up for me."

"Then how did you resolve the fee issue?" I asked.

"Jonah thought he could run Brian's playbook on the Russians' accounts. I told him not to, that he was playing with fire. You get caught stealing money from a rich person, you go to jail. You get caught stealing money from a mobster, you get a bullet in the head."

"Except this time, it was a bullet in the chest that went into my daughter's head."

Jake's whole body sagged. "Yes. Maybe if they'd hired a professional, it would've been a shot to the head and Amelia would've survived. But the nephew wasn't that good of a shot. He's lucky he hit Jonah at all."

"Lucky?" I asked coldly.

"Unlucky," he corrected. "The whole situation was unlucky. The person the nephew should've come after was me. He thought he had."

"But why would he have been looking for you in Santa

Veneta?" Aunt Maddy asked. "Didn't the Russians know you lived in LA?"

"I never told them where I lived for obvious reasons. And the nephew wasn't bright enough to figure out someone like me would never post a picture of himself online. That's how they found Jonah."

"Jonah didn't post pictures of himself online. He hated social media." He thought it was a huge waste of time. I didn't disagree, but I still used Facebook to keep up with old friends. Although I never posted photos of us. Mainly I just commented on other people's posts.

"There was a picture of him on the firm's website. We think the nephew must've gotten a screen grab of me from a security camera then ran a reverse image search and found Jonah that way. It was a stupid move because what he really wanted was the missing money, and once he killed Jonah, he had no way to get it. But the nephew was not what you'd call a strategic thinker."

I collapsed onto the chair I'd been pacing in front of. I felt depleted. Jonah and Amelia were dead all because the management firm thought putting photos of their executives on the company website would make them seem friendlier? It was hard to believe something so innocuous could have such deadly consequences.

Of course, this wasn't a random killing. For the nephew, it was personal. Not only did he think Jake was stealing from him but usurping his power too. He probably enjoyed killing Jonah; enjoyed getting his revenge. He never knew he killed the wrong man.

"I'm so sorry, Grace," Jake said. "I never meant for any of this to happen. You have to believe me."

I did believe him. But that didn't mean I could forgive him. Not yet, and maybe not ever. But I could acknowledge his pain.

I'd lost a husband and a child, but Jake lost his brother, his best friend, and his only family. "What happened after the police killed the nephew?"

"What do you mean?" Jake asked.

"I realize you couldn't just go back undercover because the Russians thought you were dead, but what happened with the investigation? Are they all in jail now?"

"No. Once my cover was blown, the investigation ended. It had to."

"Why? Couldn't the FBI just send someone else in?"

"That's not how it works, Grace. This was a multiyear effort with a lot of resources behind it."

"Then after all that effort, why didn't the FBI finish the job? Why didn't they go in and arrest everyone? Surely, you had some evidence."

"The goal was never to arrest the low-level guys. We wanted to take down the entire organization. Since we could no longer do that, the decision was made to focus our resources elsewhere."

"Focus your resources elsewhere? What the hell does that mean?" It sounded like corporate doubletalk to me.

"Exactly what it sounds like. We shifted our focus to a different criminal organization, one that didn't know my face. I believe you saw some of their files when you were snooping in my apartment."

"Is that why you had a jeweler's loop and all those articles about diamonds? I thought maybe you had a secret girlfriend and were thinking of proposing."

Jake let out a laugh. "No, I'm not even dating anyone at the moment. But if you ever want to know anything about the four Cs, I'm your man. And that is as much information about the investigation as I'm going to give you, so don't ask."

"I don't care about that investigation. I care about this one."

"There is no active investigation of the Russians at this time, which isn't to say there won't be in the future."

"Don't give me that bullshit. You may or may not investigate these people ten years from now. Not good enough, Jake. Jonah died trying to help you take these guys down. Maybe you can just walk away and move on to something else, but I can't."

"And what is it you think you're going to do?" he asked.

I didn't know. But I knew what I wasn't going to do—and that was nothing.

Chapter 45

My meeting with Jake's boss was scheduled for Tuesday afternoon. We both had conditions. Mine was that Jake not be there. Jake's boss's condition was that I give the FBI the flash drive. I promised to bring it with me to our meeting, but that didn't mean I was going to hand it over to him. I wanted something in return. I wanted them to re-open the investigation into the Russians.

I had just gotten onto the freeway on my way to LA when MJ's school called. They requested I come to the school as soon as possible. The assistant assured me MJ wasn't hurt, but that's the only information I could pry out of the woman. I pulled off at the next exit and drove directly to the Winston Academy.

When I arrived in the lobby of the administrative building, I found MJ sitting on the sofa watching a video on his phone.

"What happened?" I asked. He had no visible bruises and there were no bloodstains or rips in his school uniform khakis or white button-down shirt, so I didn't think he'd been in a fight. He just looked upset.

MJ slipped his phone into his pocket. "Sorry, Grace. I messed up."

I sat down next to him. "Messed up how?"

Then the door to the head of school's office opened, and Anna Cooper stepped into the hallway. "Good morning, Ms. Hughes, I'm glad you could come on such short notice. Let's talk in my office."

"Okay," I said and stood up. I still had no idea what we were supposed to be talking about.

MJ stood up too, but Ms. Cooper told him she wanted to speak to me alone, so he sat back down.

I waited until Ms. Cooper had shut her office door and sat down behind her large mahogany desk before I asked, "Would you mind telling me why I'm here? All your assistant would tell me was that I needed to come to the school right away."

"There's been an incident," she said calmly and with authority. I could see why the Winston Academy Board of Trustees had hired her.

"What kind of incident?" I asked.

"An altercation. MJ verbally abused his teacher and another student in class this morning."

I assumed "verbally abused" was a private school euphemism for cursed at. "You mean he used the F-word?" I wasn't sure even I was allowed to say the word on campus.

Ms. Cooper nodded. "Among other things. I'm not going to repeat what he said. I'll let you discuss that with MJ directly. I asked you to come here today so we could discuss the situation and to inform you of the consequences."

"Detention?" I asked, hopefully.

"We're putting MJ on probation. If he has another outburst like today's, then we will ask him to leave the school."

"You would kick him out of school over an argument?" I had to wonder if there was some racial profiling going on here. I doubted if Olivia Baylor cursed at a teacher, they'd consider booting her from the school.

"It was more than an argument, Ms. Hughes, it was a verbal assault. And I will say out of character for MJ. I realize he's only been with us a few months, but until today, his behavior's been exemplary. I want to believe today's outburst was a reaction to his distress over the upheaval in his living situation. My hope is once that's been resolved, his behavior will return to normal." When I didn't respond, she said, "You are aware he's leaving his current foster home?"

"Yes," I said, "but I didn't think MJ knew yet."

"He found out this morning. His homeroom teacher said she could tell he was upset when he arrived, but when she asked him what was wrong, he wouldn't tell her. After the incident with his English teacher and the other student, our security guard brought him to my office. I insisted he account for his behavior and that's when he told me."

This was my fault. I'd intended to ask Aunt Maddy about fostering MJ and Sofia again on Sunday, but then Deena called and all my plans went out the window. What I couldn't figure out was why Tim and Richard had told MJ without at least giving me a heads up. "MJ's current foster parents are great," I said, "but they just adopted a baby and they're a bit over-whelmed."

Anna Cooper nodded. "It was MJ's social worker who told him. He was very upset, understandably, and even more so because he heard it from his social worker instead of his foster parents. I think he felt betrayed."

Jesus, I really messed this up for everyone. "Let me talk to him. It wasn't their fault. It was mine."

"It's not just that," she said. "His new foster home is in Solana and the bus doesn't go that far. I told him if transportation was the only issue, we would work with him to try to find a solution. But we cannot tolerate these kinds of outbursts. It's not fair to the teachers and the other students. I've spoken to our school counselor. She thinks MJ would benefit from outside counseling to help him deal with his emotions in a more constructive manner."

"I've offered to get him a therapist before, and he wasn't interested. But I'll talk to him again. I'll tell him it's a condition to him staying at the school."

"That would be helpful," Anna Cooper said. "We're all very fond of MJ and would like to see him remain at the school, but we can't ignore his behavioral issues."

I nodded and Anna Cooper stood up. She walked me back to the lobby where MJ was waiting. As soon as he spotted us, he put his phone away and stood up. MJ raised his eyebrows but didn't speak.

"We'll talk in the car," I said, and he followed me out of the building.

We walked through the school parking lot in silence. MJ waited until I drove out of the school parking lot and onto the main road before he spoke. "Are you mad at me?"

"No," I said. His behavior was unacceptable, especially at school, but he had every right to feel angry, including with me. "I'm just sorry we're in this situation."

"It's not *your* fault."

"Actually, it is. Partially. I'm the reason Tim and Richard didn't tell you."

"You knew?" he asked, his voice rising.

"I found out Saturday. The only reason they didn't tell you was because they were hoping you and Sofia could move back in with me. Thank you for not telling them about my suicide attempt, by the way."

He shrugged. "I thought it was a secret."

"It was, but not anymore. I explained the situation to them and told them I had to talk to my aunt. I'm one hundred percent sure that's why they didn't tell you themselves—they were waiting for me to get back to them. So, if you're going to be angry at someone, the person you should be angry with is me."

But he didn't seem angry, or even upset. He seemed resigned. "Aunt Maddy don't want us no more?"

"Don't think that, MJ. I didn't even ask her yet. But I'll do it tonight, I promise." Even as I said it, I wondered if it was a promise I could keep. I was supposed to be driving down to LA to meet with Jake's boss. I'd called on the way to MJ's school to tell them I was running late, and we pushed the meeting to late afternoon. Then I looked over at MJ and realized I needed to reorder my priorities. Jonah and Amelia were dead and MJ was alive. The meeting could wait.

Chapter 46

I DROPPED MJ at Tim and Richard's house without stopping in and drove directly to my aunt's house. I found her in the kitchen chopping carrots to add to a chicken, which was sitting in the roasting pan.

"What are you doing here?" she asked, wiping her hands on a kitchen towel. "I thought you were meeting with the FBI today."

"I rescheduled. We need to talk about MJ and Sofia."

"Why? What's happened? Are they okay?"

I took her worrying as a hopeful sign. "They're fine. Sort of. Long story short, they need a new place to live."

Aunt Maddy didn't immediately say yes. But it took less arm twisting than I thought it would. First, I had to point out the odds of MJ and Sofia getting a great foster home three times in a row were astronomical. Then I reminded her even if Maria did regain custody, which was not guaranteed, it didn't mean she couldn't maintain some sort of relationship with the kids. I pointed out she had told me Maria had been friendly to her when she supervised their visit. There was no reason to think she couldn't work something out with her as I had with Tim and

Richard. And when Aunt Maddy asked what would happen if Maria refused, which I had to acknowledge she had the right to do, I promised I'd get Alex to convince her. Then I reminded her Alex was the one who said MJ and Sofia would be better off living with us.

I didn't know which one of my arguments persuaded her or if my arguments had no effect and she was just feeling guilty. Or maybe it was seeing Sofia again last week. Whatever it was, Aunt Maddy agreed and that's all I cared about.

I immediately texted MJ the good news, then called Tim and told him too. He invited my aunt and me over for dinner tonight. The roasted chicken would have to wait.

But the FBI waited for no one, apparently.

Chapter 47

Assistant Special Agent in Charge Roberto Diaz called me while we were eating dinner at Tim and Richard's house. I figured if he was calling it must be important, so I excused myself from the table and took my phone outside.

"Is there any way we could meet tomorrow instead of Friday?" he asked.

"Probably." I had a court appearance scheduled for tomorrow. It was my final status meeting for Janelle. But I was sure if I called her and told her I couldn't make it, she could easily find an associate at her new law firm to take my place. "Why?" I asked. "Did something change?"

"A little birdy told me the SEC's going public with their investigation into your husband's former firm this week. I want to make sure we have our ducks in a row before it happens."

"But I thought Brian wasn't involved with the Russians." That's what Jake had told me.

"He wasn't," Agent Diaz replied. "We believe his death may have been a suicide. The medical examiner found no evidence of foul play, and if Sullivan knew the SEC was closing in on him, it's possible he would've wanted to end things."

"Then why the rush?"

"Because if we're going to end up in a turf war with the SEC, we want to be able to say we have an active investigation too."

AGENT DIAZ WAS SHORTER than I'd imagined he'd be when we spoke on the phone. He was about my height, but broad and muscular. That was apparent even though he was wearing a suit. The buttons on his white shirt were strained at the chest, not the belly, and I wondered if he'd been a wrestler in his younger days.

Agent Diaz led me into a generic conference room whose wall of windows overlooked the 405 freeway. At this hour the cars were still moving. If we kept this meeting short, I might be able to make it out of the city before the freeway turned into a parking lot.

We sat down at the end of a long conference room table where a laptop was already sitting open. "May I see the flash drive?" Agent Diaz asked

I pulled the flash drive out of the zippered compartment of my purse, but I didn't hand it over. "Can you tell me a little bit about your investigation? Obviously, I'm not asking for anything classified."

Agent Diaz glanced down at my clenched fist where the flash drive remained, then back up at my face. He kept his expression neutral. "What would you like to know?"

"Jake told me you shut it down after Jonah was killed." I assumed Jake had told his boss about our conversation on my aunt's patio and that I refused to give him the flash drive. Presumably, that's why Agent Diaz asked me to bring it to our meeting today.

I had no reason to distrust Agent Diaz. But when I woke up

this morning, it occurred to me the timing of the supposed imminent announcement from the SEC seemed awfully convenient.
Was I being paranoid? Maybe. But when I checked all the business news sites, I didn't see any mention of Brian Sullivan or the
management firm. After learning Jake had lied to me for years,
his boss concocting a story about an imminent SEC announcement to get me to hand over the flash drive didn't seem so
farfetched.

"We had to shut it down," Agent Diaz said. "The Russians
thought they'd killed Jake and we wanted them to keep thinking
that."

"I understand that," I said, "but why did that mean the
investigation had to end? Couldn't you just send in another
undercover agent?"

Agent Diaz stared at me for several seconds before he
replied. "Ms. Hughes—"

"Grace," I said. "You can call me Grace."

"Call me Robert. And let me say how very sorry I am for
your loss. What happened to your family was a tragedy."

I swallowed hard and pushed aside all thoughts of Jonah
and Amelia. Now was not the time. "Thank you."

He looked down before he answered, as if weighing his
words. "There are a lot of factors that go into investigative decisions. We have limited resources."

I stayed silent and stared at him—a trick I'd learned from
Dr. Rubenstein.

"We don't want to expend our limited resources on low
level players," he continued. "The goal is to take down the
entire organization. We want to decapitate it, not just nip at its
tail."

"I know. Jake told me."

"Then he must've also told you we couldn't move forward
without a source on the inside."

"I understand that, but why not send in a new agent? The Russians still needed someone to launder their money."

"It's not that simple."

I stayed silent again, waiting for him to fill the void, but this time he didn't. I decided to try a different tactic. "You said on the phone you were reopening the investigation."

"Yes. Although that is somewhat dependent on what we find on that flash drive," he said, nodding to my still clenched fist.

And there it was—the hedge. I was right to be suspicious.

"You already know what's on it. I told Jake everything." Not of my own free will, but I doubted Jake had told his boss how he'd gotten the information out of me.

"We still need to have our digital forensics team examine it," Agent Diaz said.

He held his palm out to me, but I ignored it. "Assuming the information on the flash drive is helpful, what does a new investigation look like? Do you place another undercover agent in their organization?"

"I understand your interest, Grace, but I'm afraid I can't share that information with you. It's confidential. I'm sorry."

"You shared confidential information with Jonah. Or Jake did."

Agent Diaz shifted in his seat. "What Jake did was...a bit unorthodox."

"You mean he broke the rules?"

"He didn't follow standard procedure. But once your husband became involved, he agreed to be a confidential informant."

"Okay then make me a confidential informant."

Agent Diaz folded his arms across his chest and stared at me. "Other than what's on that flash drive," he said, nodding again to my still clenched fist, "do you have any information about this organization? Anything your husband might have told you or that you discovered after his death?"

Of course, I didn't. Until recently, I didn't even know this organization existed. So I was as surprised as Agent Diaz by the words that next flew out of my mouth. The idea had just popped into my head. Afterwards I wondered if maybe Jonah's spirit had been with me in that conference room and whispered the words into my ear. When I mentioned that theory to my aunt later that evening her response was, "No, Grace, you've just lost your mind."

She wasn't the only one who came to that conclusion.

Chapter 48

"HAVE YOU LOST YOUR FUCKING MIND?" Jake's voice bellowed out at me from my car's tinny speakers. I was sitting in traffic on the 405 freeway barely a mile north of the Federal Building where the FBI's LA field office was located. Obviously, Agent Diaz hadn't wasted any time filling in Jake on our meeting.

"It's the only way," I said.

"No, Grace, it's not the only way. The FBI has undercover agents who are trained to do this kind of work. Yours truly, for example."

"I won't be working as an agent. I'll be a confidential informant, just like Jonah."

"Yeah, and we both know how well that turned out. Are you trying to be next? Is that what this is? Another suicide attempt? Because there are easier ways to kill yourself if that's your goal."

I sucked in my breath. That was a low blow, even for Jake. "I'm not suicidal anymore, but thanks for your concern."

"Then what is this, Grace? Revenge?"

"Justice. Without it the whole system falls apart. There needs to be accountability. Actions have to have consequences."

"There have been consequences. I made sure of it. The nephew's dead. What more consequences do you want?"

"The same consequences you want. The same consequences the FBI wants. I want to take down their whole damn organization."

Jake let out a harsh laugh. "How? By getting yourself killed?"

"No, by representing them. As their attorney I'll have access to all sorts of information."

That was what I'd proposed to Agent Diaz. I'd work for the Russians as their attorney while simultaneously being a confidential informant for the FBI. Agent Diaz had laughed at me too. But he was willing to hear me out to get the flash drive. He still hadn't agreed. Not yet. But he was considering it.

When I arrived at my aunt's house three hours later, her reaction was the same as Jake's, but with less cursing. Aunt Maddy knew me better than Jake though. She knew once I'd made my mind up about something, it was pointless to try and stop me.

She sighed. "It's the tater tots sit-in all over again."

I smiled at her across the kitchen table. It was just the two of us. MJ and Sofia, who'd moved back into my aunt's house earlier in the day, were both upstairs. Sofia was asleep, and MJ who was supposed to be finishing his homework, was probably playing an online game with his friends. Aunt Maddy had fed the kids dinner earlier and heated up the leftover roasted chicken for me when I'd arrived.

I set down my fork and knife and picked up my wineglass. "I guess my personality was formed at ten years old and I'm never going to change."

"What are you going to tell your mother?" Aunt Maddy said. "She's not going to be happy about this."

"Nothing," I replied. "It's called *confidential* informant for a reason. The only person I'm telling is you."

"You're going to have to tell her something. You know she'll ask."

I'd already thought about this on the long drive home. "If this happens, and it's still an if"—Agent Diaz was clear on that point; he hadn't agreed to anything yet— "I'm going to tell her I've decided to continue with my law practice on my own. She's not going to ask me who my clients are or what kind of legal work I do for them. All she cares about is if I'm dating again."

Aunt Maddy chuckled. "That much is true. When will you know?"

"I'm not sure. Agent Diaz said before he'd even consider this, he needed to talk to another one of his confidential informants. He said in order for this plan to work, we would need that person's help."

"Who's the other confidential informant?"

"I have no idea. But if he, or she, agrees then I'll have to meet them. I got the impression we'd be sort of working together in some way."

Aunt Maddy pursed her lips. "I don't like this. They're asking you to trust your life to someone you've never even met."

"They're not asking me to do anything. This was my idea, remember? And if the FBI trusts this person, then shouldn't I?"

"I guess," she said grudgingly.

"Agent Diaz told me my plan has no chance without this person's help. I can't just show up on the Russians' doorstep with my business card. Someone they trust needs to recommend me. And for my own safety, Agent Diaz wants this person involved."

"How is this even legal?" she asked. "What happened to attorney-client privilege?"

"It's not absolute. You can't hire a lawyer to commit a crime for you and then claim all your communications with that lawyer are privileged. It doesn't work that way. There's a crime-fraud exception. But I still don't want to have to testify against them because if I did I'd have to go into Witness Protection, and that's not something I'm willing to do. Testifying will be the other confidential informant's job."

Aunt Maddy shook her head. "I know you're doing what you think is right, but I worry about your safety, Grace."

"You don't think I'm worried? Trust me, I am. But what's the alternative? Maybe someday the FBI prosecutes these guys and maybe they don't? I can't live with that. I can't live with knowing they're alive, walking free, enjoying their life while Jonah and Amelia are dead. This is the only way I can ensure justice is done."

Chapter 49

I'D JUST RETURNED to my office—I'd been across the street trying to negotiate a month-to-month lease with my landlord Mike Murphy—when my phone buzzed. It was from a blocked number and I almost didn't answer it, but now that I was unofficially co-parenting MJ and Sofia again, I felt like I no longer had that luxury. What if it was one of their schools? What if someone was hurt? What if they needed me? I couldn't ignore phone calls anymore.

"I was about to hang up," Agent Diaz said when I finally answered.

"Sorry, I didn't know it was you. Your number's blocked."

"You should expect a lot more calls from blocked numbers in your future."

"Why?"

"Because that's how the Russians operate."

"Oh my god!" I screamed. "That's great news."

"That is not the reaction I normally get when I ask someone to be a confidential informant," Agent Diaz deadpanned, "especially in an organized crime case."

"Sorry, I'm just really excited."

Agent Diaz sighed.

"Am I not allowed to be excited? Is that against the rules?"

"I'm concerned you do not fully appreciate the danger you're putting yourself in. This is not going to be like it is in the movies."

"I know that," I said, tamping down my enthusiasm. "But this is something I have to do."

Agent Diaz sighed again. "And that is the only reason I'm agreeing to this. Well, one of the only reasons."

"What's the other?"

"My confidential informant, the one I told you about, has agreed to testify. In the past he'd been unwilling."

"That's great. How did you get him to change his mind?"

"I didn't. You did. Apparently, you two already know each other."

"You mean Jake? How is that going to work when the Russians think he's dead?"

"Jake is an undercover agent, not a confidential informant."

I was glad Agent Diaz couldn't see me rolling my eyes. "Then who?"

"Alex Perez. He told me you two are well acquainted. He also said you were the most persistent person he'd ever met, and unless I wanted you hounding me about this for the rest of my life, I should just agree to do what you wanted now and save myself the trouble."

I collapsed onto my office couch, my mind reeling. "I can't believe Alex is a confidential informant for the FBI. I thought he was a drug dealer."

"He is," Agent Diaz said. "Many of our confidential informants are criminals. We don't often get upstanding citizens such as yourself, who volunteer to put themselves and their families in danger."

"Wait, my family's in danger?" I thought I was only endangering my own life.

"Again, Grace, I cannot stress enough that this is real life, not a movie. That said, there would be no reason for anyone to go after you or your family because if all goes according to plan, no one is ever going to know you were the source of our information. Alex is the one who will testify against them."

My mind immediately jumped to MJ and Sofia. "What about Alex's family?"

"He doesn't have any, or no one close."

"He has a sister, and a niece and nephew."

"They don't live with him and, according to Alex, he doesn't see them that often. If he stays away from them, they should be fine."

"And what if he doesn't stay away? What if they want to see him?"

"Grace, if you want to back out of this, just say the word. No one will think any less of you."

"Did I say I wanted to back out? I'm just saying I want to keep everyone safe."

"There are no guarantees."

"And if I don't do this? Will you still re-open this investigation? You didn't seem to be doing much before I offered to be an informant."

"We didn't have the flash drive before. We do now. But I'm not going to lie to you, Grace. Even with the information on the flash drive, without an informant and someone willing to testify, we don't have enough to prosecute. I'm not saying the investigation wouldn't proceed, but it would be at a much slower pace."

"How slow?"

"I can't quantify it for you," Agent Diaz answered testily. "In light of our current staffing shortages and the present administration's focus, an investigation of this type would likely be moved to the back burner. I'm not saying it won't ever happen, I'm just saying it's not the agency's highest priority at this particular moment in time."

"But you'll move it to the front burner if I agree to be a confidential informant and Alex agrees to testify?"

"Yes, but you are under no obligation to do this. I want to be really clear on this point. This is dangerous work. I will protect you as much as I possibly can, but I cannot guarantee your safety or anyone else's."

"I understand. But will you guarantee that if something goes wrong, you will protect my family and Alex's family too?"

"I will do everything in my power to keep you and Alex and both of your families safe."

"Then I'm in," I said. "I want to take these bastards down."

A Note from the Author

Thank you for reading *The Lies We Tell*. I sincerely hope you enjoyed it. Book 3 in the series, *The Truth of It*, will be released on August 22, 2023.

If you enjoyed this book, please consider leaving a review. While word of mouth is still the best way to discover new books in my opinion, those online reviews help too! If you could spend a few minutes leaving a review at Goodreads or your preferred online retailer I would be extremely grateful.

Thank you!

About the Author

Beth Orsoff is an Amazon bestseller and the author of twelve novels ranging from romantic comedies to domestic suspense. You can find information about all of Beth's books and contact her at www.bethorsoff.com. While you're there you can sign up for her mailing list and she'll send you a free ebook!

Made in the USA
Las Vegas, NV
03 November 2023

80191557R00142